MW01133856

Shades of Deception

Fighting in Shadows, Volume 1

Piper Dow

Enjoy the story!

Piper Dow

Published by Piper Dow, 2018.

SHADES OF DECEPTION

First edition. December 15, 2018.

Written by Piper Dow.

Dedication

To M, J, and K – pursue your dreams!

Special thanks

To Bob, Mom, and Aunt Frankie, my strongest and most supportive cheerleaders, thank you.

CHAPTER ONE

K elly dabbed carefully at the congealed blood around the gaping hole in her shoulder. She wiped away a clot of red to reveal the waxy yellow of flayed skin below and grimaced. The blood dripping from the gash in her forehead oozed down past the corner of her eye. She closed her eyes and resisted the urge to reach up and touch her face, then stood back to get a good look in the mirror. It looked good –– really authentic.

"Wayne, you're still too pretty from behind. Let me help," she said, wielding a cosmetic sponge covered with Cadaver grey paint and a spray bottle of stage blood.

A radio in the main room pushed out bouncy tunes through the surround sound system, but in here they could still converse. The two were in a side room in the family's walkout basement, which Kelly had long ago outfitted with a long table on one wall, an iron rod on the wall for hanging things up, and deep shelves along the end wall. When she was younger, she had used the room for crafts and painting, but a few years ago she'd added three large mirrors over the long table and started dabbling with costumes and special effects.

Wayne's close-cropped head was sporting a nasty-looking spike sticking out. They'd argued over its placement – Kelly thought it should be coming through the side of his jaw so that it left no doubt that it hadn't hit his brain, but Wayne had argued that it made it much harder to move his mouth, and he wouldn't be able to eat while in make-up. Secretly Kelly had been counting that as a pro for the jaw placement, but since it was Wayne's head, he did have final say.

"Whaddaya think?" asked Wayne, holding up a brown plaid flannel shirt in one hand and a faded green sweatshirt in the other. "Just this t-shirt is going to be too cold."

Kelly eyed him in the mirror with irritation.

"Wayne, look. In the mirror – look. What do you see?" She watched Wayne's eyes in the mirror, knowing he wouldn't get it. When his eyes met hers in their reflection, she grimaced and pointed at the spike in his head.

"Oh, right! Well, wait, the flannel one is a button-up, I can wear that one, can't I?"

Sighing, she nodded. "It can't be clean, though. We have to mess it up, and this blood won't wash out afterward, so if you like the shirt, you won't want to wear it. If you don't care, then I don't care."

She watched the conflict in his face as she finished dabbing on the stage make-up, alternating bits of Cadaver grey with Moss green to ensure that the skin around the wound was mottled and aged properly. Tiring quickly of his indecision and recognizing that covering his arms meant less work for her, she said, "I have a grey zip-up sweatshirt in the car you can use. It's already filthy from riding under the tire last week when I had that flat."

Wayne tossed his shirt aside. "Excellent. Are we ready, then?"

"Almost. I just want to add these," she said, moving to the seat at the mirror and picking up a package. She pulled out the contact lenses she had just gotten in the mail that afternoon. "I was afraid they wouldn't come in time. These are going to totally finish this costume!"

Wayne watched with a small frown on his face as she pulled the skin down from one eye and carefully placed a cloudy lens on her eye, then blinked rapidly to settle it into place. She repeated the process, looked intently into the mirror, then turned to give him a better view. The lenses had no irises – just a cloudy fog covering the lens so that they gave the appearance of the wearer being dead.

"Perfect! Come on, Rick and John said they'd be ready by 7. It's almost that now, and Mom said she wants pictures before we go."

Wayne led the way, stumbling and thumping his way loudly up the stairs. He was breathing loudly through his mouth, sounding like he was sucking air through a wet tube.

"Gross, Wayne," Kelly prodded him in the shoulder.

"I'm just getting into character," he said, grinning back over his shoulder at her.

She wrinkled her nose at him but said no more.

Wayne nudged the door into the kitchen open and shuffled his way into the room. He moved slowly, blocking the way through the door. Kelly pushed her hands past him, grasping and grabbing in front of him as though trying to get her share of whatever might be in the room. She couldn't see around him, and couldn't hear anyone over the music they had forgotten to turn off downstairs. She nudged the door open wider and side-stepped into the kitchen, from behind her brother.

The kitchen was empty. Wayne turned to look at Kelly, eyebrows raised. Kelly shrugged.

"I don't know where she is; I'll check upstairs," she said. "Go shut the radio off."

A quick check of the upstairs produced no Mom, and no Dad, either. Kelly ran down the steps and met her brother in the living room.

"I found this on the counter near the stove." Wayne shoved a small square of paper toward her. On it, written in her mother's hurried writing, were four words. "Be back soon, Mom."

Kelly's brow furrowed as she reread the note. "Well, that's weird. She could have just called down to us." She looked up at Wayne in time to see him shaking his head.

"Remember the radio?"

"Oh, right. Well, we'll just take some pictures with my cell phone. It's not our fault she's not here, and I don't want to be late," Kelly said.

They moved into the kitchen where the lighting was better. Kelly used the timer on her cell phone camera, propped it up in a coffee cup so the lens was exposed, and they staged a few photos using the kitchen knife set as props. She took a couple of close-ups of Wayne and had him snap a couple of her before they headed out the door.

"Let's take your car so I can message these to Mom on the way," Kelly said.

Wayne grabbed the sweatshirt from Kelly's trunk, then jogged to his car on the street, unlocking his car doors with the remote as they approached. Kelly slid into the passenger seat and clicked the seatbelt in with one hand, her other hand already busy tapping away on the message to her mother.

As Wayne drove the familiar route, Kelly scanned her newsfeed on her cell. She reached forward and turned the volume down so she could speak.

"Jess said she's going to be there, too. Did you know?"

Wayne nodded, still keeping time on the steering wheel with the radio. "Yeah, she said she might go with Robin, who might go with Adam. Or maybe it was Gregg. Somebody she's into this week." He seemed to notice Kelly watching him. "It's fine, Kel. It's not her fault her father's a jerk, but it wasn't going anywhere anyway."

Kelly looked intently at Wayne until his eyes met hers. As he turned his attention back to the road in front of them, she nodded and turned back to her newsfeed.

"Ok, but if I catch you acting like a moonbat tonight I'll pour a drink in your lap," she said. The threat was a standing joke between them –– a promise to help get out of a sticky situation by making an even bigger scene.

They pulled into the parking lot near the student center. Wayne maneuvered into one of the last spots in the lot and cut the ignition. Kelly was already unbuckling her seat belt.

"Rick said they'd meet us out front. Come on," she said, climbing out of the car.

The sidewalk and lawn were already crowded with people. Fog hung near the ground, spilling out of the shrubs at the edge of the grass. Lights flashed from sets of stands set up near the front of the student center, and loud music pulsed from speakers set out across the front of the building. A large banner stretched across the front of the building announcing the "Zombie Apocalypse Party." Kelly and Wayne made their way toward a large tree to the left of the student center, winding their way around other zombies and those who had decided to attend as survivors. Kelly knew Rick and John were among the survivors since Rick had said he was planning to attend as his namesake, the main character from a popular zombie show.

She found them standing under the tree. Rick wore brown pants and an open tan shirt over a white t-shirt – his TV counterpart was a Sheriff. He had been growing his beard for nearly two weeks for this party and had a disrespectable scruffiness to his brown hair. He had a toy cap-gun strapped to his belt, along with what looked like a chef knife from a kitchen set. John wore a pair of filthy jeans and a denim shirt with the sleeves ripped off. He had fashioned a primitive bow from a tree limb and piece of rope, which he had slung over his back along with a few short sticks with feathers glued to the end to resemble arrows.

"Not bad, not bad," Kelly teased, walking around the pair and critically assessing their costumes. She reached out to touch the blade of Rick's knife. "Not too sharp, here, buddy. How many skulls is that going to be able to penetrate?" She tried to raise one eyebrow, but the make-up on her forehead had a Botox-like effect. She settled for putting her hands on her hips and frowning in mock severity.

"Hey, considering that you're the zombie, I would think you'd prefer a dull blade!" Rick laughed. "Very realistic, too, I must say.

How long did it take you to do all this?" He reached out to touch the hole she had put on her shoulder, withdrawing red fingertips. "Yuck."

"The blood and everything took about an hour today, but I'd already made the prosthetic pieces. Oh, and my clothes, I worked on those yesterday," Kelly said. She glanced down at her jeans, which she had stained liberally with inkberries and mud from the yard and her sweater – a pick from the thrift store that she'd ripped the shoulder out of to ensure the bite would show through.

Rick looked toward Wayne, who was looking around at the students milling on the lawn. "You up for this?"

Wayne turned back and grinned. "Of course I'm up for this! Look at all these lovely corpses – what could be better?"

Kelly rolled her eyes, then realized the others couldn't tell because of her contact lenses. They were making it darker than it was, but otherwise, she didn't think they were impeding her vision much.

"How'd they manage all this fog?" she asked. "That's pretty cool. Dry ice?"

John motioned her to follow him as he moved toward the low hedge behind the tree. "Yeah, they've got it in buckets spread around in the bushes. The buckets have paint roller grids on them to keep anyone from accidentally touching the ice."

John was also a student in the theater department, though he was focused more on directing movies than creating the special effects to pull them off. He had just spent the past month helping to plan the party and coming up with the decorations. Kelly thought he had a right to feel proud - it had turned out fantastic.

The party was planned around showing the season opener scheduled to come on at 9, but the season finale from the last season was going to show at 8. A screen was hung along the far wall, with a projector connected to the audiovisual equipment to project the show. Another table along the right side of the room was lined with colorful little plastic cups, with what looked like a trash can behind the table. Displayed on an easel next to the trash can was a circle divided into different colors, all matching the colors of the cups on the table. Kelly veered toward the display, drawn by the cheerful colors, and saw that it was set up for a drinking game.

People were already lining up to spin the wheel and get their colored cups. Kelly hesitated. She didn't mind an occasional wine cooler at a beach fire during the summer, but she didn't think it was too smart to drink on campus.

Rick had no such qualms. "I'm in," he said, joining the line.

Wayne reached toward his pocket, but Kelly reached out and touched his arm, shaking her head once. He turned his gesture into an elaborate backstretch. Kelly hid her smirk as she turned her attention across the room. She motioned with a nod of her head toward another group of people gathering. Along the other wall were three dart boards outfitted with zombie cutouts. Students were taking turns aiming suction-cup dart guns at the boards. The noise level was nearing a level that was making it impossible to carry on a conversation. Wayne motioned with his hands that he planned to join the shooters. Kelly nodded.

She watched him walk across the room before turning back to find Rick watching her. "You going to babysit all night?"

"I'm not babysitting him, Rick. That's not fair," she said, leaning in to make sure he could hear her. "But you know that if I brought him home wasted, my parents wouldn't forgive me, and I'd never get to come to another event. You think it's worth that?"

Rick grinned but put his arm around her shoulder. "I'm just messing with you." He reached the table and took his arm from her shoulder to pull out his wallet. He passed forward his cash and reached to grab the wheel. He spun, and the arrow landed on blue.

Rick raised his shot glass in mock salute and turned back toward Kelly. John was right behind Rick and spun the wheel to red.

• • • •

THIRTY MINUTES LATER Rick had already made several trips to the shot table, and John was on his third trip. The noise level in the room, which had quieted when the show was first turned on, was rising. The soundboard techies were muting the sound and playing music during the commercials. Wayne had dragged a seat over to their cluster during the first set of ads.

Wayne leaned toward Kelly suddenly. "What did Mom say about the pictures?"

Kelly shrugged. "I don't know, I haven't checked." She dug her cell from her pocket. She tapped a button and swiped the front of the phone. A small frowned teased at her mouth. "It doesn't even say she saw them yet."

The music faded out as the show returned from commercial break.

"I'll call home between the shows," she said, turning her gaze back to the screen.

She tried to focus on the action on the screen, but now that she was reminded of her parents' strange absence at home she felt distracted and on edge. Her parents were dependable. Boring, maybe, but dependable. They didn't disappear without a word. They didn't stay out for hours when they'd only left a quickly dashed off note. They certainly didn't leave the house after supper on a Sunday night when they both had work early in the morning.

By the next commercial, Kelly already had her cell in her hand. She stood casually, motioned that she would be back in a few, and moved toward the side of the room where the doors to the bathrooms were. Glancing back she saw Wayne in conversation with John, who was laughing boisterously. Kelly saw several girls waiting outside of the restroom, so walked out the front door instead. She waved vaguely with one hand to a girl who called out her name, but kept walking.

She quickly dialed her home phone. Surely her mother had just not looked at her cell phone and was sitting home watching television on the couch. When the answering machine came on after the fourth ring, Kelly hung up and stood looking down at her phone. She hit the messaging app with her thumb and saw that her mother had still not seen the photos she had sent on the way to the party. She dialed her mother's cell. When the call went straight to voicemail, Kelly hung up and dialed her father's cell. That call went straight to the automated voice telling her that her dad still hadn't bothered to set up his voice mail. Kelly wasn't surprised since he hated using a cell phone, but she had thought it might be worth a try.

An arm wrapped around Kelly's waist. She jumped and whipped her head around to see who was at her side. "Rick!"

"Hey, watcha doin? You disappeared on us, Kel. Kelly," Rick said.

Kelly took a breath through her mouth to avoid the smell of the alcohol on Rick's breath.

"Just trying to figure out where my parents are. They're not answering any of their phones," she said.

"Oh, so now you have to watch out for them along with Wayne, huh? Poor Kelly, you have too many people to keep track of, that's what's wrong with you," Rick said. He tugged her toward the door with his hand, which she had tried unsuccessfully to remove from her waist. Kelly allowed herself to be steered back into the room but resumed the effort to remove Rick's hand from her waist.

"It's just weird, them not answering. I messaged my mom while we were driving here, and she hasn't even seen the pictures yet. Hey, how many shots are you up to?"

"I don't know, a few," Rick's diction was slurred.

"Wow," Kelly said. She smiled sweetly up at Rick's expression, which was stuck between trying to figure out if she was admiring him or insulting him. "This explains so much."

The music faded out as he opened his mouth to say something, and Kelly shushed him. "Ooh, it's back on. This is the last ten minutes, right? Let's see what happens –– it's got to be a cliffhanger!"

They moved back to their seats. The room was getting more crowded as people who hadn't bothered to show up for the replaying of the last episode started coming in to see the season opener. Twice Kelly bumped into people, apologizing profusely as one girl spilled the contents of her cup onto her friend. Rick stepped on the edge of her shoe, causing her to bump a third person. She reached her seat gratefully and sank onto it. Rick leaned toward her to say something, but Kelly put a finger up to his lips and pointed at the screen, settling back in her own chair. Managing regular Rick was easy enough, she'd been doing it for years, but managing tipsy Rick was proving to require a little more finesse.

As the characters on the screen ran to escape a herd of zombies, Kelly looked around again, fighting irritation at the haze the zombie contacts threw in front of her eyes. The lights were dimmed so that the show would be easily visible projected up on the sheets, but her contact lenses really were impeding her vision more than she had thought they would. She turned back to find Rick watching her with a smirk hovering about his lips. He leaned toward her again.

Kelly stood. "I think I have to get in line for the restroom; I might be a while. Save my seat?" she smiled sweetly again at Rick.

Laughing softly at the look of confusion on his face, Kelly headed for the far wall again. This time she did get into line for the bathroom. She pulled her phone free from her pocket and swiped her thumb across the screen again. This time she had a notification for a voicemail from home. Kelly looked at the number of girls in front of her in line, then glanced around the room. It was way too loud to hear a message in here, but the music had also been loud outside. She decided to wait until she got into the bathroom to listen to it.

"Kelly, we have to go," Wayne appeared at her elbow. His voice was steady but urgent. "I just talked to Dad. I'll tell you on the way, but we have to go."

Her stomach lurched a little. Wayne's face was tight, his jaw clenched, and his eyes were already looking at the doors.

"Let me just tell Rick we're leaving," she started, but Wayne cut her off.

"I already did, that's how I found you. He's a few shots over his limit, I'm guessing. Really, Kel, let's go," he said, tugging her out of line and toward the door.

CHAPTER TWO

"Dad called," Wayne said. He pulled his keys out of his pocket and hit the remote to unlock the doors. "He said he left you a message. He said we had to come home now, and he would explain everything when we got there."

Kelly glanced at her brother as she climbed in on the passenger's side. She still had her phone in her hand. As Wayne pulled the car out of the lot, she swiped the screen and hit the speaker so that her Dad's voicemail would play. Reaching forward, she shut the radio off.

"Kelly, this is Dad," she heard his voice fill the car, tense and urgent. "I need you and Wayne to come home as quickly as you can. Drive very carefully. Do not speed, do not do anything that would get you into trouble, just come home. I don't want to scare you, but if it looks like you are being followed, go back to the center of town and send me a text. I'll get to you as soon as I can. Stay together, no matter what.'"

Kelly looked at Wayne, startled. He had both hands gripping the steering wheel tightly, but was driving the speed limit. She hit replay, and they listened to the message again.

"Is that what he sounded like when he talked to you?" Kelly asked.

"I don't know," Wayne said, sounding fretful. "It was so loud in there, I was having a hard time hearing him, and I had to yell to ask him to repeat stuff. He said to get you and come straight home, said to drive very carefully, and said he would explain when we get there. Do you think something happened to Mom? Why wouldn't she call?"

"I don't know. I mean, something is definitely up. What about that 'make sure you're not being followed' bit – what's with that?" Kelly suddenly twisted in her seat to look out the back window and scanned the sidewalks and intersection they were passing. "We're not, are we? Being followed?"

"How would I know?" Wayne's voice climbed higher as it got louder. "This is crazy, Kel!"

Kelly kept watching the street behind them. Her throat felt tight, and her hands were shaking. She gripped the console and the back of her chair, willing her panic back down. She watched as a white SUV pulled out of the parking lot at the grocery store onto the street behind them. The SUV followed them three blocks, but then turned left into a driveway. Wayne continued driving straight.

"Go by Jess' house, instead of Thomas Street. Just in case. Whatever this is, if someone thought we'd come home like usual they could wait for us on Thomas Street. If we go a different way," Kelly trailed off when Wayne turned his head to look at her.

His jaw was clenched, and his hands shifted and tightened reflexively on the steering wheel. He nodded curtly in her direction, then turned onto Johnston Drive instead of continuing on Main Street. Kelly turned her head this way and that, looking all around them as they drove around the back way to their house. She could hear her heart pumping in her ears. The car rounded the corner near Jess' house. Jess' dad's car was parked on the road in front of the house, the only vehicle out of place on the street. Wayne glanced at it without comment as they passed, flicking his eyes quickly up to the house and then back to the road in front of them.

Taking another turn at the next intersection, Kelly peered up and down the street looking for anything that seemed out of place. Mrs. Horstach's porch light was on three houses down the street. Mr. Ross was walking his dog, Nestle, down the sidewalk. Nestle was busy sniffing around in the fallen leaves that had gathered at the end of the Bailey's driveway. Lights glowed from windows up and down the street. Things looked normal.

Turning onto their own street, Kelly's attention was caught by the glint of the streetlight on the windshield of a minivan pulled over on the side of Thomas Street. She squinted at the vehicle, trying to decide if it was suspicious or not. At a distance of a quarter mile away, she couldn't be sure. She pointed at the van. Wayne was squinting at it, too.

"This is crazy," she whispered. "Let's just get in the house."

Nodding, Wayne pulled the car into the driveway. He drove around to the side of the house where Kelly's car was parked, pulling up onto the grass next to her car. There wasn't enough room for four cars in the driveway; usually, he left his parked on the street in front of the house, but Kelly was glad that he'd parked closer to the house. Dad's call had her spooked.

They jumped from the car and quickly ran up the steps to the side door. It opened before they reached the top stair and their dad appeared in the doorway. He looked harassed and urged them in quickly. He closed the door almost on Wayne's heels.

"You made it without any problems?" He asked tersely.

"Yes." "No trouble." "Dad, what's going on?" Kelly and Wayne interrupted each other in their eagerness to find out what had happened.

"Sam called Mom," Dad started. He motioned the two to follow him into the living room as he continued. "She was talking really strange; not making a lot of sense. She said she was on the bus, she would be at the station by 6:45, and wanted us to come get her." He neared the coffee table, which was covered with papers – some of them printed, some of them covered in Sam's neat handwriting. "We got there just after the bus drove off. We looked around and didn't see Sam, but then Mom saw her cap on the ground near the side of the building – you know the one she wore all summer, with the purple dog on the front? We went around the corner and saw a couple of animals fighting over something on the ground. We got a little closer and saw one of Sam's red sneakers on the ground. We ran toward them, and the animals ran away, and there was Sam on the ground. Mom's at the hospital with her now."

He was gathering all the papers together as he spoke, stashing them into Sam's backpack, which was on the floor near the couch. Kelly noticed a duffel bag on the table, and her dad's gun bag on the floor between the couch and the coffee table.

"Dad, what else is going on? Why did you tell us to be careful coming home? Why did you think we might be followed?" Kelly could feel her shoulders tense and wiped her sweaty hands on her pants. "Dad?"

He had walked near the window and was standing off to the side, carefully moving the curtain forward an inch or so so that he could look outside.

"There was a minivan up on Thomas Street, just parked across the street from Jameson's house," said Wayne. "We couldn't tell if it was weird or not."

Kelly sank into one of the chairs, her attention divided between watching her father and looking around the room. In addition to the duffel bag, gun bag, and Sam's backpack, there were a couple of blankets, Wayne and Kelly's jackets from the front closet, and Sam's laptop gathered together.

"Some of what Sam was saying on the phone to your mom had to do with seeing people change. Mom thought maybe she had taken something, or been slipped something – she sounded like people who are on LSD or acid. At the bus station, she was still conscious when we found her. She kept trying to talk to us, and Mom kept trying to get her to calm down. I finally promised her I would look at what she had brought – her proof she kept saying we needed to see, and she calmed down enough to go in the ambulance."

Dad was still looking out the window toward Thomas Street. He glanced back at their faces, then out the window again.

"Mom went with Sam in the ambulance. I followed them in our car. I had Sam's backpack, her laptop was in it. That's all she brought with her. I checked her bag to see if there were any drugs or anything in it that would explain, well, any of this. I found some pictures she had printed out. I – I thought at first she had done something to them, played with them on the computer or something, but some pictures looked like the animals that were attacking her at the bus station. Mom and I saw those – and I know we weren't on anything."

His voice was raw, emotional. He stepped back from the window and covered his face with his hands, pressing his fingertips into his eyes before lowering his hands to his hips.

"I waited until we were sure that Sam is going to be okay before coming home. Mom stayed with Sam; we didn't dare leave her alone. I need you both to come with me. I don't," he paused, taking a deep breath and exhaling it slowly. "I don't think it's safe here. This doesn't feel like it can be real, but I am not willing to risk taking chances." He looked at Wayne, then at Kelly. "Sam thinks one of those animals is her roommate Jill's boyfriend. She thinks he might have killed Jill."

CHAPTER THREE

K elly woke slowly, feeling the ache of sleeping on the floor in her hips, her shoulders, her back. She knew before opening her eyes that it was early; the gray light of the pre-dawn hours had not yet given way to the amber glow of sunrise. Her head was stuffed with the ideas she had read in Sam's notebook last night, and her dreams had been filled with werewolves and dragons and creepy, greasy men with missing teeth and bad haircuts.

Kelly opened her eyes and sat up, wincing. She needed coffee, a big coffee. And maybe some Excedrin, too. She pushed her hands through her hair, trying to rub the cobwebs from her mind. Wayne was asleep a few feet away. His lips parted as he breathed out, little "phht" sounds escaping every few breaths. Turning the other way, Kelly saw the sleeping bag her dad had used still spread on the cot, but no Dad.

She lifted her head quickly, eyes darting around the tiny room. The cot in the corner, the round table with two chairs in front of the window – all were as they had been last night when they arrived, with the addition of Sam's notebook and laptop laying on the table. Rising to her knees, she could see a piece of paper on the top of Sam's laptop cover. In one less than graceful movement, Kelly lurched forward to grab the paper from the table.

"Gone for coffee and breakfast stuff. Do not open the cabin door, do not leave. Will be back soon, Dad."

Kelly sighed. Her parents were going to have to knock this cryptic note-writing stuff off. She could feel the panic that had risen in her throat beginning to subside. Running her tongue over her teeth, she pursed her lips in a grimace as she felt morning fug and realized she hadn't brought her toothbrush with her. She glanced at her watch and saw that it was nearly 5. The lone window in the cabin faced south, a beautiful view in the evenings, but not very helpful this morning. Kelly looked down at Sam's notebook. The tiny hand-writing in the dim lighting would make her headache worse. She grabbed the laptop instead and crossed the room to sit on the cot, leaning against the wall, pulling her legs up and tucking her feet into her dad's sleeping bag. She flipped the laptop open and hit the power button.

Waiting for the laptop to load its operating system, Kelly tried to make sense of last night's events. Mom and Dad went to get Sam from the bus station. They saw Sam's hat and found her in the al-ley being bitten by some big coyotes or jackals or something. Dad had tried to describe what they had seen, but his voice would falter, and his eyes kept getting a panicked look. It sounded like Sam was in rough shape – she'd had to have surgery to repair some damage from the bites. Dad got choked up when he tried to tell them that, too.

They had gathered some clothes and things they might need overnight, then hurried to his truck by the side of the house. Dad had carried Sam's bag with her laptop in one hand and his handgun in the other, not getting into the truck until they were both in and the gun bag was stowed at Kelly's feet in the back seat. He pulled out of the driveway without turning on the headlights and drove out the way Wayne had driven home from the party, away from the van on Thomas Street. Only when they had taken a left at the end of the street had he switched the headlights on. Kelly had watched out the back window but hadn't seen any movement from the other end of the road.

They had driven longer than was necessary to get to the cabin. Dad took roads that led toward the city at first, then doubled around and took a meandering route to get to the cabin. His eyes were con-tinually flitting between his mirrors and the road. He sat upright, barely touching the seat back. Kelly recognized his long, slow exhales as attempts to stay in control of the situation and bit back her ques-tions. Wayne stayed quiet for so long that Kelly was surprised he was still awake when he finally broke the silence that had overtaken the car.

"So, um, Dad. What do you think is going on?"

Dad glanced at Wayne, then back at the rear-view mirror and back at the road. He seemed to be weighing his words.

"Sam thinks Jill's boyfriend, Mark, killed Jill and is trying to kill Sam. She thinks that if he followed her home, that none of us are safe. I'm not sure what I believe yet, but I know something attacked her, and if that means there's even a possibility that you guys are not safe, we need to get some space while we figure things out." He glanced in the rearview mirror again, but this time at Kelly and not at the road. "We're probably all fine, and in a few years we'll end up laughing at this, but for now, let's just be safer than sorry, okay?"

Kelly had nodded without saying anything. Wayne had looked back over the seat at her, looking like he wanted to ask more questions, but at her nod, he sighed and turned back to look out the window into the night.

When they finally reached the cabin, Dad made them wait in the truck while he checked it out first. It was his father's cabin, but they used it every year for fishing, hunting, and for a few weekends that Mom billed, "getting away from life as we know it." In addition to a small bathroom, the cabin had just two rooms – the second one had bunk beds stacked along the walls, but after taking off their zombie makeup and spending a couple hours of reading and discussing Sam's notes last night, they had all fallen asleep in the main room.

With the laptop booted, Kelly plugged in earbuds, selected a playlist from Sam's downloaded tunes, and turned her attention to the photos Wayne had moved to the desktop. The first few were of friends at a party Sam had attended. Jill was in three of the pictures. Her long, dark hair framed a face that was thinner than Kelly remembered from last summer. She had used a heavy hand to apply her makeup. Kelly carefully appraised the look, deciding that Jill could pull it off. There was something about her, though –– were her shoulders held too high? Was there a shadow to her smile? Kelly's brow puckered as she tried to puzzle it out. Of course, she reasoned, it could also just be that a photo represents a split second in time, and she was looking at the images with suspicion already planted.

Kelly opened the email program, and with a few taps, had attached the photos and Sam's journal pages to an email and sent it to herself. As long as she was going for suspicious, she might as well go all the way. Her focus moved to the others in the photos. There was a guy with his hands around Jill's shoulders in two of the pictures. This must be her boyfriend, Mark. He was unshaved, though his beard was sparse. There was a pinched look to his mouth, Kelly thought. His eyes were very dark –– Kelly enlarged the photo on the screen to see if she could see their color, but with the shadows, the best she could do was "dark." She supposed if they were blue the color would be easier to detect, so mentally labeled them as brown. His dark hair was on the longer side, curling up around his ears and collar. He wore a plaid buttoned front shirt over a black t-shirt, with faded jeans. Kelly could see nothing particularly memorable about him.

There were a couple of other people in the background of the photos. In one of the pictures, one man appeared to be looking soberly at Jill. There was no smile on his face, unlike the rest of the party-goers, who all seemed to be laughing at something near the picture-taker. Kelly quickly scanned the other pictures from that same date, but he was only in the one.

Kelly shrunk the party photos and opened the other two pictures that Wayne had saved to the desktop in the photo editing program. She played with color saturations and lighting levels to see if she could identify any editing work, but everything looked original. The photos were dark and grainy, taken in low light with no flash. One showed five figures – one of which looked like it was being dragged on the ground. That figure was wearing the dress Jill had worn in the party photos, although Kelly couldn't see her face in the picture. Two of the shapes were crouched low and looked like dogs tugging on the body. The other two were standing; their faces were in shadow but did not look like anyone Kelly had ever seen before. In fact, they didn't look like people at all – their bodies did, but their noses were elongated, and their teeth took up a much bigger area than Kelly had ever seen before.

The second photo was even more unnerving. Two figures were standing in front of a building, under an amber street lamp. They were smoking, the glow from the ends of their cigarettes visible in their hands. One face, though somewhat cloaked by the cigarette smoke, gave Kelly the impression of a werewolf, but different. The second face was staring toward the camera.

CHAPTER FOUR

"Kel!"

Kelly started, snapping her head up and looking wildly around. "What? Holy crap, Wayne, don't scare me like that!" She pulled the earbuds out of her ears.

"Jeez, Kel, I've been trying to get your attention," Wayne sat at the table and chairs in front of the window. Light streamed into the room –– the sun was clearly past the horizon now. Kelly checked the clock on the laptop. It was nearly 7.

"Where's Dad?" Wayne asked.

Kelly pushed the laptop to the side on the cot and disentangled herself from the blankets. "He left a note. Says not to open the door, he went to get coffee and breakfast and would be back soon, but I woke up a while ago and he was already gone. He should be back by now if that's all he went for." She crossed over to the table and sat in the other chair.

Wayne nodded, tousling his hair. He glanced at Kelly, then away, at the laptop. Kelly waited. Minutes ticked by.

"I put some photos on the desktop."

Kelly nodded. "I was looking at them now."

"Could you tell," he began, but Kelly's head shake cut him off. "They weren't edited?"

"Not that I can tell."

More silence. Wayne glanced again at Kelly, then back at the laptop.

"Was it her? Was she," his voice trailed off instead of finishing the question.

"It was the same dress. That's all I can tell for sure from the photos," Kelly said. She watched his face. She usually let him take the lead, ask the questions he was ready to hear answers for, but his plodding pace was too slow as a memory swam to the forefront of her mind. "Wayne, do you know what 'skinwalkers' are?" He shook his head, but then slowed and cocked his head to one side.

"Is that what Sam was talking about last month when she was home?"

"I think so. I video-chatted with her last week. Remember all that stuff about legends and fables she was talking about when she was home?"

Wayne nodded, still looking quizzical.

"She told me last week that some of the legends are real. She said she had seen something – she said it was a 'skinwalker' that some of the legends are about," Kelly said. "Jill came in the room while we were chatting and Sam changed the subject. I was going to say something, and she made those googly eyes at me –– you know, when she wants you to be quiet in front of Mom and Dad and makes those eyes? Like that. I had forgotten about it, but now," Kelly trailed off, too.

"You think the pictures might be of those? Of skin walkers?" Wayne asked.

Kelly shrugged. "Maybe. It'd be worth finding out, don't you think?"

Wayne gave a non-committal shrug. He glanced again at the laptop. "Kelly, I know Mom and Dad saw those things, and I know Sam has pictures of them, but," he faced Kelly straight on, his words spilling over each other now. "The things she wrote – some of that sounds like Sam was cracking up! C'mon, sneaking around and being afraid to use the internet at home? Thinking her food was all going bad and throwing everything in the fridge away? Does that sound sane to you?"

Kelly shook her head slowly. "No, it actually reminds me of someone with schizophrenia. In my psych class, there was a girl who has schizophrenia, but she takes medication for it. She said before she got diagnosed she had hallucinations that made everything taste like it had blood or metal in it. People with schizophrenia sometimes can think they're being watched, and they have trouble keeping things straight on what's real and what isn't." Kelly thought, rubbing her forehead, trying to see which pieces fit together. "But Wayne, Sam was being followed – she was attacked after she came home! And she does have those pictures of things that Mom and Dad saw. How likely is it that some of what she saw and wrote about was real, but some not?"

Kelly shook her head more firmly. "No, I don't think Sam is crazy. I don't know what is going on, but I don't think she was losing it."

Wayne squinted one eye and chewed the inside of his bottom lip. "But, Kel, seriously, what are we talking about here? People don't just turn into animals – werewolves don't exist. They can't!"

He stood abruptly, pushing back the chair with his legs and just catching it by the top to prevent it from tipping over. He strode to the cot and picked up the laptop, then carried it back to the table. He used the touchpad to open Sam's journal program and scrolled, looking for a specific entry.

"Say this wasn't Sam, wasn't someone you knew writing this," he said. "Tell me what this sounds like. Here. 'Overslept again this morning and missed church. Head feels like it's filled with Jello, so hard to make simple things make sense. Found the bread on the counter instead of in the fridge, but Jill hasn't been home in two days. No dishes in the sink. Poured a glass of milk, but couldn't drink it – curdled. Just bought it yesterday. I left the book about the Mi'kmaq tribe on the coffee table yesterday when I took a nap, and when I went to find it later it was missing. Found it this morning in the bathroom – I don't read in the bathroom.'" Wayne glanced up at Kelly to make sure she was listening. "The earliest of these kinds of entries is from right after Sam came home last month. She seemed okay, then, right? But listen to this one: 'Really wish Jill was here to talk to, maybe she could help me figure this out, but if she were here then probably Mark would be here, too, and then I couldn't talk to her about it anyway. I keep seeing these people that no one else seems to see. I was walking down the street and saw someone in the store window following me. When I turned to look, there was no one there. I was sitting in the library and felt like I was being watched, but I looked all around and didn't see anyone. I was at the grocery store and saw a man out of the corner of my eye. I thought it was David, Mark's friend from the party, so I was going to say hey, but he had turned a corner –– and when I got to the next aisle, he wasn't there. I kept an eye out, but he wasn't in the whole store. When I left to walk home, I felt like I was being watched again, and I felt like it was him. And that's crazy. I feel like I'm losing my mind.'"

Wayne looked up again and brushed his hair out of his eyes. "Kelly, she said it herself. She thought she was going crazy."

"Yeah, Wayne, ok, but then explain the things that attacked her at the bus stop. Dad said something was biting her, and he can't even bring himself to describe whatever the things were accurately, so you know there was something horrible about them. I'm just saying, Sam didn't end up in the hospital because she was imagining things," Kelly said. "I'm not saying you're wrong – I'm not," she pushed on before Wayne could interrupt, trying to forestall an argument. "Look, let's look at this from all angles. Let's pick it apart. But let's not decide something is or is not without looking at everything, okay?"

The sound of tires crunching on gravel outside silenced them both. Kelly imitated Dad's movements from the night before, standing to the side of the window and peeking out.

"It's Dad," she said, motioning to Wayne to open the door. "He's got Dunkin'!"

CHAPTER FIVE

Wayne opened the cabin door as Dad was reaching for it, trying to balance the cardboard tray of coffee cups and a bag of pastries in one hand to free his other for the doorknob. He broke into a tired smile as he saw them eagerly waiting.

"I was longer than I wanted to be, I'm sorry," he said, setting the tray of coffees down so that he could hand out cups. He pulled out a cup, read the markings on the side, and handed it to Kelly. "Caramel swirl, regular. So this one is French vanilla," he added, handing another cup to Wayne. "There are muffins in the bag."

He sank into the chair that Wayne had vacated and leaned back, bringing his own coffee to his lips.

"I went to the hospital. Sam is doing all right. They've got her on IV antibiotics, in case whatever that was that bit her was diseased. She was running a low-grade fever last night by the end of the shift, so they're watching her. Her arm looks like it will probably heal okay, but the leg is going to have a pretty mean scar."

Wayne, mouth full of cranberry muffin, tried to say something but stopped. He chewed to clear his mouth, then started again.

"Dad, we've been trying to put things together," he started.

Kelly cut across him. "Let's hear what else Dad has to say, first," she suggested.

Irritation flashed across Wayne's face, but he shrugged and took another bite of muffin.

Dad looked back and forth at the two before speaking.

"Listen, I don't want you two getting in the middle of this. We don't know what is going on, but we know something is -- and it's not good. I don't want you getting hurt, too."

Kelly slapped her hand down on the table. "We're already in the middle of this! Look at where we are!" Kelly struggled to control her voice. "We had to leave school early last night and come home to pack up stuff and drive half-way through the night to hide in a cabin so we could be told not to open the door until you come back, and you think we're not in the middle of this? Do not tell us we can't help figure this out!"

Dad blew out his breath slowly. "You're right. I'm sorry. But if you help, you have to do it my way, and be extremely careful. We don't know what we're dealing with."

Kelly and Wayne both nodded, watching him attentively.

"Ok, so what else did you find out this morning?" Asked Wayne.

Dad described driving to the hospital, following a circuitous route again and continually checking to make sure no one was following him. He had driven past the house, just to see what was going on, and saw the same van parked on the side of Thomas Street.

"I was thinking of getting someone else's vehicle to drive past that van to see if it's there legitimately or what, but I put that on hold," he said.

He had driven next to the hospital, parking in the employee lot and watching the cars in the lot before walking to the entrance.

"I don't know if there's a reason to think someone might be staking out the hospital or not, but better to be," he said.

"Safe than sorry," Wayne and Kelly both chimed in, smiling. It was a familiar mantra.

"Right," he said, not smiling. "I talked to security before going up to Sam's room. The guard had an interesting story from the night. I don't know if it's related, or not. There was a commotion in the ER that security had to respond to. A handful of kids all dressed up like zombies were brought in – a couple had to have their stomachs pumped because of alcohol poisoning."

Kelly felt Wayne glance at her but refused to turn her attention.

"While the zombies were milling about, trying to scare patients, a couple of people tried to get past the security door," Dad said. "They didn't look like zombies, and the guard said they didn't look like college kids, but nowadays you can't really tell. They didn't get access to the rest of the hospital, but if they were trying to get up to Sam, they might be back."

"Other than the fact that strange things are going on in our family, what makes you think they were trying to get up to Sam's room?" Asked Kelly.

"The guard said they were talking between themselves about getting a laptop before they tried opening the door. They told the guard they were trying to get homework notes from a friend," said Dad.

Kelly nodded. She bent and rifled through Sam's bag, pulling a notebook and pen toward herself. It might help sort things out later if she wrote them down. She turned to a fresh page and wrote in a column, "Sam attacked. Van on Thomas Street. ER zombies. Someone trying to get a laptop, homework notes."

As she wrote, she asked, "You didn't happen to hear the names of any of the zombies, did you?" She rubbed her forehead with her left hand and tried to keep her voice casual.

"No, the guard didn't use names," he said, watching her pen move across the paper. "Mom said Sam didn't have a restful night. Neither did Mom. They've got a bed made up for her, but you know hospitals – they're in and out of the room checking things all night. Plus, she doesn't know everything that's going on. I haven't told Mom everything we found in Sam's bag, but I did tell her she needs to be alert to anything strange, which of course made her anxious about sleeping. If you really want to help, you guys could take turns staying with Sam so Mom can get some sleep today."

Kelly nodded.

"So, Sam's going to be okay, then?" Wayne asked.

Dad considered the two of them before speaking. "We don't know what bit her, but the doctors were able to close the wounds. She did wake up after the surgery, but she's been asleep all night since then. There's a lot we still don't have answers to, but yes, I think she is going to be okay."

"Ok, so how are we going to handle this?" Kelly started talking as she thought things through. "You want us to go to the hospital and stay with Sam so Mom can get sleep –– is she going to come here? We all came together. We only have your truck. Shouldn't we get our vehicles? But then there's a bigger risk of being followed, if there's anyone following. But if we don't get our vehicles, it means a whole lot of all of us sitting around doing nothing because we're stuck without vehicles."

"Dad?" Wayne broke into Kelly's stream of conscious monologue. "What about the police? Shouldn't we talk to them?"

Dad's mouth twisted as he considered Wayne's questions. "Well, on the one hand, that's a good idea. Sam was attacked. On the other hand, it looks like she was attacked by animals. Mom and I aren't sure what we saw, but it would be hard to describe them as people, and the wounds looked like animal bites. If she was attacked by animals, it'd be something for police to watch out for, but nothing criminal, and animals are not likely to keep trying to get her, or her laptop. Everything else we're suspecting is based on Sam's pictures and journal, none of which is likely to convince anyone else that something is going on."

Dad sighed. "But if there really is something going on, the police have far more resources to deal with it than we do. It's just – I know this sounds like we're crazy." Dad looked at Kelly. "To your point, yes, I guess we are going to have to get your cars. If we go to the house first, you guys can get a car and go to the hospital. I'll call the police and ask them to have someone meet us there. That way they'll be able to talk to Sam, too."

They made quick work of tidying up the cabin, not bothering to repack everything since they would be returning in a few hours. Kelly stashed the notebook and Sam's laptop back in her bag and slung it over her shoulder. The police might want to take a look at it, and she didn't really want to let it out of her sight. If someone really was trying to get their hands on it, leaving it unprotected was not a good idea. With that thought in mind, Kelly turned to look at the room before closing the door, trying to make a firm imprint in her mind of where everything was. She wanted to be able to tell if anyone did try to look around while they were gone.

CHAPTER SIX

D riving back to the house took twice as long as it usually did after a weekend of fishing. Dad drove North on Rte. 1 to get to Tremont Street and took that around town before taking Main Street back through town to get home from the opposite direction. Kelly and Wayne decided to drive Wayne's car to the hospital so that Kelly could keep an alert eye on their surroundings.

"Don't go into the house," Dad cautioned. "I don't want to take the time to check it out every time we come near it, and I don't want you going inside unless I check to make sure nobody is in there waiting."

Kelly had been hoping to go inside to grab her pillow and some Excedrin but didn't argue. They were heading to a hospital; she was sure she'd be able to find some medicine for her headache there. Tonight she would sleep on one of the bunks in the back room so her body wouldn't be as sore when she woke up.

They approached the neighborhood, and Dad took a right onto Thomas Street.

"We may as well see if that van is still there," he said.

It wasn't. Kelly felt an odd sense of letdown.

"What in the world?" Dad muttered under his breath as he turned down their street. White streamers of paper hung from tree branches and draped over the shrubs near the road in the front of their house. Their house had been T-P'd.

As they drove slowly closer, Kelly noticed silly string had been shot at most of the windows and the mailbox, and both Wayne's car and hers had been slathered with shaving cream. She looked up and down the street. None of the other houses had been hit, just theirs.

"Don't touch anything yet," said Dad as he parked the truck on the street in front of the house and they all got out. He turned to Wayne. "Do you have anything to tell me about this?"

Wayne opened his mouth wordlessly and then closed it again. He looked thunderstruck.

"Seriously, Dad? I've been with you and Kelly since yesterday afternoon!"

"Could this be payback? Have you done anything to anyone else?"

Kelly knew Dad was thinking about the Parker's house that Wayne and a few of his friends had toilet papered a month ago. They had been caught, and the police made them clean it all up and then expanded their efforts to clean up the whole street, going so far as to make them dig the empty fast food cups and used nip bottles out of the weeds at the edge of the road before deciding they had made sufficient retributions.

"I don't know anything about this," Wayne said through gritted teeth. His hands were balled fists shoved in his pockets.

Dad nodded. "Okay, then. Let's just head to your cars and check them out."

He scanned the neighborhood as he spoke, scrutinizing the shadows under the trees and at the sides of houses. He motioned them forward.

Wayne reached his car first. He cupped his hands around his eyes and leaned forward to peer into the car, making sure he didn't touch the window. A moan of anguish escaped him. Dad grabbed his hand as he reached for the door handle, preventing him from opening the door. Kelly looked inside quickly, then ran to assess the damage to her own car. Wayne's car had been trashed; his car seats were slashed, and a gaping hole in the dash indicated where his stereo had been. The inside of her car, however, had been left undisturbed.

"Okay, that's strange," she said. "Aside from the shaving cream, my car looks fine."

Wayne's head was bowed, and his arms were curled around his head, with his fists near his ears. "No, no, no, no, no," he was mumbling. ""Not my car, no, no, no." Angrily he wiped his face on his sleeve and turned to face Kelly. "Let's just go, then. Let's just go."

"No. Not yet," Dad said, holding out a cautionary hand.

Surprised, they looked at him.

He slowly walked around Kelly's car, crouching down to look at the ground underneath the engine and again at the rear of the car. Reaching out one hand, he touched the grass under the motor and withdrew it, rubbing his fingers together. Moving to the other side, he repeated the motion. This time, his fingers were coated with amber fluid.

"Don't touch the car," he said. "The brake lines have been tampered with. Let's go, back to the truck. We're all going together to the hospital. You can call on your cell phone and have someone from the police meet us there."

Stunned, Kelly looked at Wayne, then back at her father. She suddenly felt like they were being watched, and copied her father's actions of a few minutes ago, surreptitiously looking in the neighbor's yards and up and down the street as they made their way quickly back to the truck.

"You see how they worked this? They trashed your car and left Kelly's looking okay so that you would take Kelly's car. If the brake lines were cut through, you'd have no brakes at all, but you'd feel that as soon as you tried stopping at the first corner. I'm willing to bet they put holes in the line so that you'd be a distance away before running out of brake fluid and getting in an accident," Dad said. His fingers were tight on the steering wheel, his shoulders tense again. "Kelly, call the police and have them meet us at the hospital. Tell them we'll be in Sam's room."

Kelly quickly opened her phone and searched for the police station's number on the internet. She didn't want to dial 911 since she was having them meet her somewhere else.

"Police, recorded line," the dispatcher answered the phone.

"I need to speak to an officer," Kelly said. "We think someone is trying to hurt my sister and the rest of us – they attacked my sister last night, and they trashed our house this morning. They destroyed our cars that were in the yard."

The dispatcher made her repeat several points of her story before telling her he would send an officer to the hospital to meet them. Kelly snapped the phone case shut to hang up the call.

"Yeah, I see what you meant, Dad," she said. She was sure she had sounded like an idiot.

"Well, that's why I didn't want you to touch anything on the cars. This way the police can get prints off of them, hopefully," Dad said.

Kelly didn't say anything. She was thinking of animals, and whether they would have fingerprints to leave.

"Dad! What time did you go to the house this morning before you went to the hospital and came back with coffee?" Wayne asked. "You would have seen this if it had been done before that!"

Dad was nodding. "I was thinking the same thing – that gives us somewhat of a timeframe that this must have happened in. The yard looked fine when I went to the house, and that would have been around 4:30 this morning. It's nearly 10 now, which is still nearly a six-hour window, but maybe some of the neighbors noticed when they went to work this morning, or didn't see it when they went to work – it would narrow it down more."

Dad didn't bother driving in a meandering path but drove straight to the hospital. "It's not like they don't know we're coming here," he said when Wayne asked about it. "They know Sam is here."

CHAPTER SEVEN

Kelly and Wayne walked quickly to keep up with Dad, whose determined stride allowed for no questions. They rounded the corner near the elevators just as a young man was stepping into one and quickly joined him before the door had the chance to close. Kelly watched as Dad went to punch the button for the fourth floor, but it was already lit. The ride up was silent, and blessedly short. Kelly and Wayne followed Dad off the elevator as soon as the doors opened, and they walked quickly down the hall and around a corner before Dad stepped to the side of the corridor and stopped. He motioned Kelly and Wayne to be quiet as he handed Kelly the backpack he'd been carrying and turned back to the intersection of the corridors. He stuck his head around the corner to look back at the nurse's desk.

He moved quickly back to Kelly and Wayne. "I don't like that guy. Sam is in room 417 – you two go there and wait until I come. I just want to make sure this guy doesn't have anything to do with any of this mess. When I come in, we'll wait for the police before telling Mom and Sam anything that happened."

Wayne nodded. Kelly glanced at the room number on the door across the hall – it was 405. They walked down the hall, scanning doors as they passed. They reached the end of the corridor before finding Sam's room. The directional sign on the wall across the hall indicated that 417 was to the right. They turned right and headed down that corridor, nodding at a middle-aged woman wearing a johnny walking with an IV pole, then found Sam's room halfway down the hall on the left.

The door was open, but the curtain just inside the door was drawn. Kelly knocked on the door as she entered the room and parted the curtain. Mom was sitting in a folding chair near the head of Sam's bed, one hand resting on the bed holding Sam's hand, with her eyes closed. Sam's eyes were closed, too. Kelly and Wayne moved quietly into the room, walking around the foot of the bed to the other side where there was more room. Mom opened her eyes and lifted her head, smiling tiredly as she met their eyes.

"The nurse was in about 20 minutes ago," she said. "She said Sam seemed more comfortable than she had all night – she was thrashing around a little in the early hours. They've given her I.v. antibiotics and pain relievers, and she just gave her something because she's running a little temp. They may have to change the antibiotics – a fever could mean she is getting an infection, and if she's getting one while they're already giving her antibiotics, they could be the wrong ones."

"Mom, you look exhausted," Kelly said. Mom's chin-length hair was sticking up at odd angles, frozen in clumps thanks to leftover hair product, and she had dark smudges under her eyes from not taking her make-up off the night before.

"Yes, well, the hospital is not the easiest place to get a good night's sleep," Mom said, stifling a yawn. "Where's Dad? Isn't he with you?"

"Yeah, he wanted to check on something at the nurse's station," Kelly said. "He told us he'll be right along."

Wayne walked over to the windows and pulled the curtain to the side a few inches, looking down at the parking lot below and at the street running parallel to the hospital.

Kelly dropped the backpack into the chair on the side of the bed and propped herself against the window sill instead of taking a seat in the chair. She leaned forward, hands on her knees. She looked up at the bags of fluid slowly dripping their contents into Sam's arm. A large bag of saline solution – Kelly assumed that was to prevent dehydration, and a smaller bag labeled "vancomycin." She figured that must be the antibiotic her mom had mentioned. Sam had on a johnny, but Kelly could see gauze and iodine-washed skin under the edge of the johnny near Sam's neck. Her arm was swathed in gauze, too, some of which was tinged with orange seeping through from underneath. Her fingers on that hand were swollen and still had iodine wash on them.

Wayne glanced out the window again, then turned his head to the doorway as they heard footsteps approaching. A hand pulled the curtain aside, and Dad stepped into the room. He was followed by a police officer.

"How is she?" Dad asked. "Is she still asleep?"

Mom nodded, looking past Dad to the police officer.

"Okay," Dad said. "Debbie, we called the police. I think this may be something bigger than I thought it was at first, and I think we may need help. Somebody was at the house this morning after I left to come here."

Mom gasped, bringing both hands up to cover her mouth. "Thank God none of you were there!"

The police officer drew a notebook out of a pocket on the side of his leg and withdrew a pen from his shirt pocket.

"I'm Officer Martin. Why don't you start from the beginning? Which one of you called the station?"

Kelly waved her hand, embarrassed. "I did, but Sam is really the beginning of the story, I guess."

Dad chimed in. "We actually don't know the beginning of this, but I can give you the part where we came in." He motioned at Mom, "Debbie got a call from Sam yesterday on her cell phone, asking her to go to the bus station and pick her up. It was just after supper; the kids were downstairs getting ready to go to their party, so we just left a note and went to the bus stop. We got there, but couldn't find Sam. I saw her hat near the side of the building. We went around the side, and saw these..." Dad's voice faltered a bit. He took a deep breath before continuing in a stronger voice, "these creatures, all fighting around something on the ground. We saw a shoe on the ground near them – we ran down the alley and the things scattered. Sam was on the ground, bleeding, unconscious."

Dad's voice faltered again, and he covered his face with his hands. Kelly noticed that his hands were shaking.

"We ran to her," Mom picked up the story where Dad had left off. Her voice was low and quiet, but level. "I picked her head up, we tried to stop the bleeding using her jacket to put pressure on. Steven called 911 for an ambulance. While we were waiting – it seemed like forever, but I think it was only 5 or 6 minutes – Sam woke up. She was frantic that we take her backpack and look at what she kept calling her proof. She wouldn't agree to get in the ambulance until Steven said we would look at it, promised that we would keep it safe."

Officer Martin had written a few notes in his notebook, but mostly he watched Dad and Mom as they talked. Occasionally his glance flickered toward Kelly or Wayne, and once or twice to Sam, still motionless in the bed.

"What did these 'creatures' look like? Did you see anyone nearby? Did it look like they had been trained to attack or anything?" he asked.

His face was smooth, impassive. Kelly couldn't tell if he was being sarcastic or thorough. Maybe he was gathering fodder for his turn at "you won't believe the nut-cases I had to deal with" tomorrow.

Mom and Dad looked at each other. Dad's mouth opened, then closed. He tried again but got no further. Mom closed her eyes.

"They looked like werewolves, but, not wolves," she said, sounding reluctant. "Like people who had changed into some kind of animal, some kind of bear, or, or, I don't know, huge dog or something." She opened her eyes and looked straight into Officer Martin's face. "Their bodies were still mostly human – they had hands. They had clothes. But their heads – their faces – I've never seen anything like them in my life."

Officer Martin's gaze passed slowly between Mom's and Dad's faces and back before he broke the silence.

"Would you be able to describe them accurately enough to work with a sketch artist?"

"We, well, we think we have pictures," Dad offered slowly.

Kelly quickly picked up the backpack and reached her hand in, grabbing the top notebook and flipping it open. She shuffled through the loose pages until she came to the two pictures that Sam had printed out and held them out to Officer Martin.

His gaze was shuttling between all of them, now, and traveling around the room as though he was half-way between not wanting to offend the crazy people and expecting someone to point to the corner of the room where a camera was hidden to catch his expression over their practical joke. He reached out to take the pages from Kelly and glanced down, then stopped and stared at the photo on top.

This photo was sharper than the pictures that Kelly had scrutinized on the laptop earlier that morning. Kelly had looked at it last night but turned to the images on the laptop this morning because she could study them better. She was too adept at manipulating images for her art to trust printed materials not to be altered.

The top picture was taken in Sam's apartment. Nearly half of the yellow flowered couch was visible in the image, as well as the counter that separated the tiny kitchen from the dining room. Kelly figured that Jill must have taken this picture; it appeared that Sam was asleep on the couch. There was certainly a head laying on the couch, and the hair color was the same as Sam's. The person was facing the other direction, though, so Kelly couldn't be sure.

Between the couch and the counter stood a figure wearing dirty jeans and a wrinkled, stained t-shirt. The man – Kelly assigned the person that detail based on the physique, not the face – looked like he was laughing. He held a half-eaten sandwich in one hand. His elongated snout was thin, and his face was sparsely covered with hair. Through his eyes, though, he reminded Kelly of Jill's boyfriend, Mark.

This and the rest of the photos that Sam had copies of were printed up on regular paper. Kelly wondered if Sam had somehow gotten hold of Jill's phone to print them up, or how she had gotten copies.

Officer Martin looked up at Kelly, then at Mom and Dad. "Where did you get this?" He flipped quickly to the second page in his hand, which held a printed image similar to the first one. "Where did you get these?" He corrected himself.

"Sam had them in her notebook," Dad said. "When she agreed to go in the ambulance, I took her backpack with her notebook and laptop. We looked at the papers she had inside when they had taken her into surgery. I didn't get to look at the stuff she had on her laptop until I went home."

Officer Martin nodded. "I'll need to see what else she had with her, and I'll need her laptop."

"There's more," Wayne said. "Somebody jacked my car!"

With a few probing questions from Officer Martin and interjections from Wayne and Kelly, Dad finished telling about the security guard's story about stopping men claiming to be students from getting into the hospital overnight and then finding their house toilet-papered and their cars vandalized. Officer Martin called the station to have a couple of officers sent to investigate the house.

CHAPTER EIGHT

Kelly paced in front of the coffee vending machine in the hallway break area. They had been sitting in the hospital room for hours, waiting. Waiting for Sam to wake up, waiting for the police to come back or call or give them an update of what was happening. Kelly had charged her phone and was able to look at the photos and files she had emailed to herself from Sam's computer, but she was getting tired and bored just sitting around, waiting.

At least Mom had gotten some sleep. She had dozed off after the police officer left, and Kelly had urged Wayne and Dad to leave the room so they wouldn't accidentally wake her. Mom had curled up in the chair that pulled into a bed, with one hand curled up under her cheek. She'd been that way for more than two hours. Dad had come back to the room and told Kelly she could take a breather.

Sam had still not woken up enough to talk to. A nurse had been in just before Mom dozed off to retake vitals. It seemed to Kelly that, even though the nurse assured them that Sam was likely just sleeping off stress, something more was going on. Who needs to sleep that much from surgery? It wasn't like she had been in a car accident and had a brain injury –– her face laying on the pillow was thinner than normal but otherwise looked perfectly healthy. Kelly had been going over the journal entries she had emailed herself while Sam and Mom dozed, trying out different scenarios in her mind to see if they explained what Sam had written.

She'd excused herself from the room to get a coffee, but instead was pacing back and forth, money still in her pocket. Kelly was glad they had called the police in, and it seemed like they were being taken seriously, but sitting around waiting for someone else to save the day was beginning to wear.

Even though she had told Wayne they needed to look at this from all angles before coming to the conclusion that Sam was crazy,

Kelly had to admit there was some validity to his argument. What she knew about schizophrenia, admittedly very little, seemed like a good fit to Sam's disorganized thoughts and insistence that someone was watching her.

Kelly looked at the vending machine without really seeing it. She felt like her brain was struggling to gain traction under the weight of too much thought. A noise from the end of the hall drew her attention. A couple of nurse's aides walked past the intersection, laughing as one told the other about dropping her coffee, her bagel, and her change from the cashier that morning and deciding to go home and start the day over. Kelly turned back to the vending machine, but a red sign hanging from the ceiling part way down the hall caught her attention, and she glanced back at it. It pointed down another hallway to what it promised was a chapel.

Kelly's legs were moving before she was conscious of making the decision to go to the chapel. A sense of relief buoyed her as she neared the room at the end of the hall. Inside were a dozen small pews all facing the back wall, where a platform held a podium with a microphone on a stand. There was a cross on the wall behind the podium. An alcove to one side of the plinth held a statue of a woman Kelly assumed was Mary, Jesus' mother.

As she walked into the room, Kelly noticed several of the pews had books on their cushioned seats. Moving into one of these, Kelly sank onto the cushion and took a deep, slow breath. She closed her eyes, focusing on relaxing her tense shoulders and trying to free herself from the tension that had built up since last night. Opening her eyes, she reached out to pick up one of the books from the seat near her. It was a hymnal. Letting it drop open, she saw the words to one of the praise songs and recognized the tune.

"Lord, I need you. Oh, I need you. Every hour I need you. My one defense, my righteousness. Oh God, how I need you." Kelly smiled as the melody played in her head. She flipped the pages in the book and found several more familiar songs to hum along with before bowing her head. "God, I don't know what's going on, but I know that you know. I'm praying for your protection - for me, for Sam, for all of us. Keep us safe, keep us whole, and help us to stand strong with whatever is going on here. Give us peace, Lord, please."

Kelly lifted her head, feeling calmer and more collected than she had when she left Sam's room. She stood, stretched her arms over her head, and turned to leave the room. As she neared the door, she saw a man pass the intersection, heading toward the vending machines. He looked familiar. Kelly had spent hours looking at his picture and wondering about him –– he was the unsmiling man from Sam's photos of the party.

Kelly stepped quickly to the doorway, her heart pounding. Who was he? Where was he going? She darted down the corridor toward the intersection. The sound from her sneakers squeaking on the tiled floor seemed abnormally loud in the quiet hall, and she slowed to keep from attracting attention. She peered cautiously around the corner. A man in jeans and a grey sweatshirt was turning the next corner, his back disappearing even as she stepped into the hall. Kelly glanced around as she speed walked past the vending machines. The brain fog from earlier seemed to have lifted – her pulse was quick, and her wits sharpened. She rounded the corner, throwing her hands up and sidestepping quickly to ward off an orderly heading for the coffee machine.

"Oh, I'm sorry!" she said, smiling awkwardly as he grabbed for her elbow to keep her from falling. "Excuse me!"

Kelly pulled her arm back and continued down the hall at a slower pace, wondering which room the man had disappeared into. Glancing at the floor, she noticed a scrap of paper. She hadn't seen it on her way to the vending machines, but that didn't mean anything. She hadn't noticed much of anything on her way there. She stooped to pick up the paper. Turning it over, she gasped. Her address was written on the small square. It looked like it had been stuck to something and pulled free

Kelly glanced up and down the hall. She didn't see anyone, though she could hear voices coming from a couple of the rooms. One room had a large group of visitors; they were talking fast and loud in Portuguese. Another room had a small child in it, crying. The door to Sam's room was ajar. Kelly moved quickly into the room and closed the door behind her before parting the curtain blocking the view of the room.

"Dad!" she whispered urgently. "Dad, I think I just saw a guy from one of her pictures, and look! I found this in the hall on the floor!" She held the scrap of paper out to him as she crossed the room to his side. "Where's Wayne?"

Dad frowned as he stared at their address on the paper. "Wayne is in the coffee shop. I asked him to bring Mom a sandwich for when she wakes up – she's not overly fond of the food from the cafeteria. You found this on the floor? Where, in this hallway? Or somewhere else? And what do you mean, you saw a guy from one of her pictures?"

"It was in this hallway, maybe 25 feet from this room. I didn't see it when I left, though, and then I saw someone I think might be the man from Sam's pictures. He was walking down this hall, but I didn't see where he went because I bumped into someone coming around the corner." Kelly was scrolling on her phone, trying to pull up the party pictures she had sent herself. "Here – he looked like this man," she said, enlarging the photo and holding out her phone so her father could see more clearly.

Dad looked at her phone through narrowed eyes, pushing Kelly's hand a few inches further away from his face. He looked back at the address on the paper, chewing the inside of his lip.

"We should make sure Officer Martin knows about this," he said. "But it could have been his note – he was here and wrote down our address on a piece of paper, and he did walk down that hallway when he left."

Kelly balled her free hand into a fist. "What about him?" she asked, pushing her phone forward again. "I'm almost positive it was him!"

"Kelly, did you see him up close, or just his back as you were following him down the hall?"

Kelly closed her eyes to prevent Dad from seeing them roll. "Dad, I was in the chapel. I was getting ready to leave when I saw him go past the end of the hall. I followed him to this hall." She opened her eyes in time to see Dad roll his. "Dad!"

"Kelly, why would you deliberately follow someone you thought was involved with what happened to Sam? And what kind of look did you get - how far away was he when he went past the end of the hall?"

Kelly gazed at the window as she tried to visualize the corridor. "I don't know, maybe 50 feet?" Dad didn't look reassured. "Ok, fine, maybe it wasn't him. I didn't see him clearly." She paused. "I didn't actually get my coffee, before. Vending machine coffee just didn't look appealing. Where did you say the coffee shop is?"

Shooting her a cautious look, Dad gave her directions to the coffee shop. "Wait, though. I want to check with the police to see if the address was from Officer Martin, but Kelly - I can't believe you would follow someone you thought might be dangerous! You need to be more careful! Something is going on and we can't be taking chances. Do you understand?"

Kelly nodded, then retreated behind the curtain and cracked open the door. She peeked out and saw a couple of young women with a baby walking down the hall. A man was closing the door to the room next to Sam's. He hurried to catch up to the women. Kelly opened her door and pulled it shut behind her as she stepped into the corridor.

CHAPTER NINE

Though she kept her eyes open, Kelly didn't catch another glimpse of the man in the grey sweatshirt on her way down to the first floor coffee shop. She stood in line behind a couple of nurse's aides and listened to their chatter about their diets. Apparently one of the girls was in a club that took pictures of one meal a day and posted it on the internet for accountability.

"I'm telling you, it's working! I've lost ten pounds already," she assured her friend.

"That is way too much effort, to me. I can't even keep track of what I eat, never mind remember to take a picture and post it. Besides, you can lie just as easy doing that as you can writing it down. Just don't take pictures of the seconds you take," the second girl laughed.

Kelly tried not to judge as the girls ordered frozen coffee slushes and muffins the size of softballs. When it was her turn at the register, she ordered her caramel coffee with one less sugar than she usually did, as penance. Turning from the counter, she saw Wayne sitting in a chair in the lobby near a low table and walked over to join him.

"Hey," she said in greeting as she sank into a nearby chair where she could see most of the open expanse of the vaulted lobby.

He was engrossed in his phone. Kelly reached over with her toes and pushed his leg lightly. He jerked his head up, sliding his phone into his sweatshirt pocket as he looked at her.

"Jeez, Wayne, calm down," Kelly said, sitting back and taking a quick sip of her coffee. "I thought Dad said you were getting Mom a sandwich."

Wayne shrugged irritably, then nodded toward the coffee shop. "Yeah, I am, but I was waiting for the line to go down."

Kelly raised her eyebrows and lifted her Styrofoam cup in mock salute.

He frowned. "Okay, fine. I didn't want to go back up yet. I'm tired of just sitting around while everyone sleeps. Someone is messing with our lives, and we're just sitting here!" His mouth twisted before he bit out, "They trashed my car, Kel! You know how long it took me to get my car set up. And I know my car is nothing compared to Sam, I know it, but I did nothing to them, and they trashed my car!"

Kelly sat forward, arms on her knees. "You wanna hear something? I just saw – well, I think I saw that guy from Sam's pictures. And I found a paper in the hall that had our address written on it. Dad thinks it might have fallen out of Officer Martin's notebook or something, but I honestly don't think so. Wayne, I think that guy is here, and it was his paper, and you're right – we're being targeted - and I don't like it one bit!"

Kelly didn't bother to mention that her car had also been vandalized. To her, the car was a practical way to get from point A to point B, and the fact that it was sporty and had a little kick in it was a bonus. Wayne had worked on his car weekends and over school breaks, buying parts from swap shops and junkyards and finishing them off with Dad's help. They had started working on the car before Wayne even had his license to drive it. To trash Wayne's car was truly hitting him in his heart.

"So, what are we going to do about it?" Wayne asked. "You heard Dad. We have to do this his way if we want to be able to help, and apparently, his way is to sit around here all day and let the police try to ferret out what's going on."

Kelly turned her head side to side as she glanced around the lobby, making sure no one was listening. "I've been thinking. We've gone through Sam's journal, we've seen her pictures. Sam's a smart girl – even if she has some sort of mental illness, which I don't think is the case, enough is going on to point to something really messed up at her apartment. I really think someone has to go to Sam's apartment and look around."

Wayne's eyes were round as he stared at her. "Dad will never agree to let us go."

Kelly nodded. "I know, you're right. But do you see another way? If the police here send police there to look around, they won't know if things are the way Sam had them or not. I was there during summer – and we know Sam. We know what is normal for her and what is not. Sure, she might have moved things around in the past couple months since I was there, but I'd know if it was something she did or something someone else did."

Kelly sat back, sipping her cup as she mulled their options. The man in the grey sweatshirt seemed to have lit a fire in her, urging her to action.

"What if," she said slowly, thinking out loud, "we let them think we are staying someplace safe for the next few days, to lay low. It couldn't be a friend's place, that could drag more people into this, and we wouldn't do that. But what if school was having a field trip, or there was a retreat going on. Would Dad think that was far enough removed from this to keep us safe?"

Wayne looked hesitant, then shook his head. "Kel, we can't lie to them like that. Not for something this serious."

Kelly nodded, knowing he was right. Besides, something like that would have already have had to be in the works for it to be believable. She mused some more.

"Well, we could take the bus up and back in the same day. They'd know something was up before we got back, but hopefully, by then we'd have some answers. If we left first thing in the morning, we'd be there by 10:30 or so. If we just act like we're going to school, we don't have to lie, and we don't have to come up with some elaborate scheme." Kelly was scrolling to find the bus schedule on her phone. "The first bus we could catch without it being suspicious would be the 6:55 –– that would put us there by 9:30." She scrolled some more. "We'd have to catch the 5:45 back, which would get us home by 8:30. It wouldn't be a lot of time, but maybe we could talk to some of Sam's other friends and see what they've been seeing."

Kelly looked up to see Wayne's expression, a mix of awe and fear. "What?"

"It's just, it really sets it home, how serious this is," he said. "I'm in. I'm just," he trailed off.

Kelly nodded. "I know. Me, too," she assured him. "I think we need to be prepared for anything. Wear good sneakers, don't bring too much we'll have to carry. I'm bringing my mace." She paused, grimacing. "Well, make that, I'm bringing my mace if I can get into the house before we go. C'mon, get Mom's sandwich and let's get back up there before they send security looking for us."

Wayne joined the line at the mouth of the coffee shop to order the sandwich. Kelly gazed around the lobby while she sipped her coffee, her brain whirling away behind a calm expression that gave away none of her apprehension. Her back to the arching stairway leading to the second story, she didn't notice the man leaning against the pillar above her. He watched until Wayne disappeared into the shop before pulling his hands out of his pockets and walking purposefully back into the hospital.

Kelly stood as Wayne walked back to her seat. She swallowed the last of her coffee. As they walked toward the corridor, Kelly veered toward the trash can near the entrance to the emergency room.

"Kelly!"

It was Mary, a girl from her statistics class. Kelly motioned Wayne to come with her and walked toward the ER.

"Are you here from the party last night? Wasn't that awful, at the end?" Mary asked.

"We had to leave just after the season opener started – what happened? We heard there were some people brought here?"

Mary nodded and began talking at the same time, enthusiastic to have a new audience. "It was terrible, and it looks like the school might be in trouble for the under-age drinking since it was a school-sponsored event. There were like, maybe 10 or 12 people brought here by ambulance. Some of them had their stomach's pumped – do you know how gross that is? Disgusting! A couple of them had to be admitted overnight. Some of them were over 21, but of course, there were some younger ones, too. Some cop's daughter was underage, she had her stomach pumped, and two of the professors' kids ended up having to be admitted for observation overnight."

"Wait, do you have any names?" Kelly asked, cutting across what looked sure to go on for another several minutes.

"Well, my friend Dan was admitted, that's why I'm here now, bringing him some clothes," Mary said, lifting a bag she held in one hand. "Did you see the girls that were dressed in zombie rock star outfits? They all had their stomachs pumped. Then, oh, do you know that guy that played baseball last spring, the one they said was heading to minor leagues? He got his stomach pumped. The cop's daughter, I already told you about, I think her name is Jen? Something like that. Professor Ostrom's son, I think, and Professor Jardin's. There was one older guy, too, nobody seemed to know anything about him, but he came in the same time as all of ours."

Kelly glanced at Wayne. He was staring, unseeing, across the hall. The cop's daughter had to have been Jess, his ex-girlfriend. Kelly hadn't seen her, but she had said she planned to go to the party. Jess' father had made her break up with Wayne, saying Wayne was a bad influence after he got caught TP-ing that house. Kelly's family knew Wayne wasn't an angel, but could also see that Jess didn't need much leading to head in the wrong direction.

"Oh, there was a guy dressed like a sheriff that got admitted, too," Mary giggled. "Apparently he sat on a knife he brought and cut......something," she giggled.

"Rick? Was his name Rick?" Kelly asked sharply, suddenly irritated at her breathy gossip.

Mary shrugged. "I don't know. Well, nice seeing you. I have to bring these to Dan." She lifted the bag in her hand again.

Kelly nodded, eyes darting around the lobby seeking the information booth. "Yeah, see you in class," she said and moved away.

"I have to see if it was Rick," she told Wayne. He nodded without speaking and followed her to the information desk. She gave Rick's name and waited while the woman looked, then told her he was in room 307. Sighing, she moved away from the desk.

"I have to go see him," she told Wayne. "You should bring the sandwich up to Mom, though." She paused, wondering if she should say something about Jess.

"Right. Don't worry about it, I'll tell them you ran into a friend, and you'll be up in a few minutes," Wayne said, moving away before she could say anything more.

CHAPTER TEN

K elly followed the woman's directions and rode the escalators up to the third floor. She looked down over the edge as she neared the second floor, marveling at how the sounds bounced around the rounded walls of the foyer. She turned the corner and walked along the open corridor to ride the escalator to the third floor, taking in the arched glass windows throwing streaks of light across the walls. The architecture of the hospital was truly astounding; she hoped the medical care was as good.

Alighting on the third floor, Kelly found a directional sign and headed down the hallway to Rick's room. The woman at the desk hadn't been able to tell Kelly how Rick was doing – she mentioned something about privacy laws, but at least he wasn't in the ICU, so Kelly figured he couldn't be too badly hurt. On the other hand, she mused, he had been admitted, so it must be more than a scratch. Kelly read the room numbers as she walked down the hall, finally slowing as she neared 307. She wiped her hands on her pants. Double checking the names on the room, she saw that Rick's name said W next to it. The other name listed had a D next to it – Kelly figured they must indicate window and door beds. Taking a deep breath and reaching forward to push the curtain aside, she walked into the room.

Kelly walked past the first bed without glancing at its resident, her eyes fastened on what she could see of the second bed around the curtain that was pulled halfway between the beds. An iv bag hung from a stand at the corner of the bed, and a heart monitor beeped softly from a monitor on the wall. Kelly hesitated, then approached the foot of the bed. A middle-aged man with a graying beard reclined on the pillow, eyes closed.

Kelly frowned. She glanced quickly at the first bed in the room in confusion. Stepping back from the second bed so that she wouldn't wake the occupant, Kelly tiptoed back to the first bed, grabbed Rick's toes under the covers, and gave his leg a little shake.

Rick's eyes flew open, and he grabbed wildly at the bars on the sides of the bed. "Whoah! Hey, that hurts!" He yelled, his other foot kicking out in Kelly's direction.

Kelly released her grip on his toes and threw both hands into the air. "I'm sorry! I'm sorry! I didn't know," she stammered. "Oh my gosh, I'm sorry, Rick!"

Rick stopped shouting and pulled himself up on the pillows, moving his foot gingerly away from Kelly. He winced, then puffed out his cheeks as he blew a deep sigh. "Hey, Kelly," he said. He motioned to the foot of the bed, where he had made room by moving his feet to the side. "Have a seat."

Kelly waited until he had pushed the button to raise the head of the bed higher then sat gingerly on a corner of the bed. "Rick, what happened?"

Rick threw his head back on his pillow and looked at the ceiling. He glanced quickly at Kelly and then at the ceiling again, marshaling his thoughts.

"After you guys blew out of there, it just seemed to get even louder and more crowded than it had been. You couldn't see the screen if you were sitting down - there were too many people standing up. I didn't even pay to join the shots game for the second half, but somehow I ended up with a few more - I don't know, that part's still a little fuzzy." Rick risked another glance at Kelly, then inhaled deeply and turned his face fully to look at her. "There were a bunch of kids messing with the punch, too, and then some of the kids out on the front started getting sick in the bushes. John was afraid they were going to be sick on the dry ice, and it would vaporize into fumes or something, so we went out to try to move the dry ice buckets, only some had already been tipped over - it was a mess, seriously. Then a guy started having a seizure inside, and somebody called the cops, and then there were cops everywhere and kids trying to run and stepping on kids who'd been out front getting sick. They hauled a bunch of kids in to get their stomachs pumped, and I think a couple were arrested."

He shook his head, disappointment flickering across his features. "I don't know, Kel. Something that seemed like such a great idea at the time turned into an absolute fiasco. Now the school's started an investigation, and they're talking about disciplining people who were involved, and then the cops were in here this morning trying to find out who provided the punch and who was drinking, and my parents are talking about pulling me out - or at least not paying for the rest of my tuition. I'm screwed." Rick was picking at the blanket across his lap. His lips twisted into a pout. "What did you hear at school today, are they canceling all school activities? The cops said they might be."

Kelly shook her head slowly. "I don't know - I didn't go to school today," she said. She watched his downcast eyes. So much had happened to her family in the last 24 hours that she was stunned to see how little impact those events had on those around her. She reached out to put her hand on Rick's leg and quickly withdrew it at his sudden intake of breath. "What happened to your leg?"

Rick closed his eyes as a self-depreciating smirk lit his face. "Oh, yeah. Remember that knife you said wasn't sharp enough to do damage to a zombie? I beg to differ. When John and I were trying to get the kids away from puking on the dry ice, one of them thought I was getting fresh with his girl. I wasn't," he said as an aside. "Seriously, what is sexy about a girl up-chucking in the bushes? Even if she did take her shirt off to keep it away from the puke - no thank you." Rick shuddered melodramatically. "So, he thinks I'm trying to go after her and grabs my knife from my belt. The cops show up as he's taking a swipe at me, so he grabs the girl and her shirt and throws the knife toward me as they're running off behind the library. I take one step, slip in the puddle of puke, and land on the knife. Believe me, it was plenty sharp."

"Oh, Rick - that is so gross," Kelly laughed. "I'm sorry I'm laughing, but leave it to you! How bad is it?"

Rick grimaced. "It cut a muscle in my shin almost clear through. They had to sew the muscle back up, and the skin, but right now I'm not supposed to walk on that leg to make sure that stretching and flexing it doesn't pull apart what they had to stitch up. Plus, I'm on antibiotics to prevent infection, thanks to all the puke that got into the wound. All in all, with all of that and you leaving early, not my best night." He looked down at the lump under the blanket that was his offending leg, then leaned his head back on the pillow again. He glanced Kelly's way again. "On the upside, with all the pain meds and the iv fluids I got, I didn't end up with the hangover I should have had. You were right about the punch, not such a great idea."

He picked his head up and looked at her again. "Wait - so what happened to you last night? Wayne said you guys had to leave but didn't say why. And why weren't you at school today? Everything okay?"

Kelly hesitated for half a heartbeat before shaking her head. "My parents were at the bus station picking up my sister - she was attacked. They had to bring her here - she had surgery, too, last night."

She wasn't sure why she was only giving Rick part of the story. Maybe she recognized, like her dad, how crazy it sounded. Perhaps she didn't want to hear Rick say the words she was sure her parents would say if they learned of her plan to go to Sam's apartment tomorrow, telling her to sit back and let the police handle things. Kelly's knee bounced up and down as she jiggled her foot, feeling a need for movement.

"Actually, I have to get going, Rick," she said, getting to her feet. "Wayne and I were getting Mom's sandwich when I heard you were in here. I have to go back to Sam's room. I hope you feel better. Do you know when you'll be getting out of here?"

Rick shrugged. "I guess I'll be here 'til tomorrow, at least, to make sure everything looks good before they send me home. And I'm definitely going home - my parents already started moving my stuff out of the dorm. If they let me go back to school at all, I'll be commuting."

He looked miserable again. Kelly felt like she was running out of oxygen - she needed to get out of the room.

"Well, maybe we can carpool. I do have to go, though," she said, edging toward the door. "I'll try to stop by to see you again if you're still here when I'm visiting Sam."

Rick nodded glumly, giving a half-hearted wave as she moved the curtain to the side and stepped into the hall.

Kelly walked away from Rick's room and rounded a corner before slowing. She leaned against the wall and pulled out her phone, thoughts spinning. If she wanted to go to Sam's in the morning, she needed to know what was going on at school so that she had a good cover story. She hadn't checked in on social media since last night on the way to the party. There was a school website she could check, too, but she would probably learn more by checking out her newsfeed first.

She started scrolling, then tapped a couple of times to sort the newsfeed by time instead of popularity, muttering insults about the general population's fondness for kittens and baby elephants. She moved the cursor to a timeframe shortly after she and Wayne had left the party, then slowly panned the results.

It looked like Rick's story was accurate, from what she could see from the postings on her newsfeed. A few of the party-goers had even posted pictures of the police scooping up friends - or enemies, Kelly snorted quietly, glad that she and Wayne had already left before the party went south. Inane posts from uninvolved friends filled space on the newsfeed. Kelly checked the timestamps and scrolled quickly to find posts from the morning, when students would have been hearing about any kind of repercussions.

"Killer party might have killed my chances at staying in school," Kelly frowned as she read Rick's post. If he wanted sympathy, this was not the best way to go about getting it. She scrolled on. "Student lounge closed indefinitely. Way to go, dead-heads. Where am I supposed to hang out when I'm supposed to be in class?" "Heard the zombies party hard - sorry I missed it!" "Professors acting like half the class isn't hung over or sleeping through their lectures rock!" "Don't think the grass will ever grow here again." The last was accompanied by a photo of the front of the student lounge, where a number of students had apparently tossed their cookies.

As entertaining as some of the posts were, Kelly hit the button to go to the school page. She wasn't going to be able to come up with a useful cover story for tomorrow if all she had to go on were partiers who felt like they'd missed out and photos of the leftovers on the ground.

The school page had an announcement pinned to the top of the feed. "Due to the irresponsible actions and behaviors of a handful of students, the student lounge will be closed until further notice. Students with any involvement with the activities of last night should expect to be contacted, and the behaviors addressed legally. Students with any information regarding the activities of last night should contact the Dean of Students office. In light of the seriousness of the situation, any future activities or events will need to be approved by the Dean of Students prior to being scheduled. Approval is not guaranteed."

Kelly reread the statement. It sounded serious, but was still vague enough for her to stretch it a little as a cover. If she told her parents that students were being asked to go to classes early because everyone was being checked before entering class, or something, it would evade suspicion enough for her to get on an early bus. Wayne should be able to leave for his school as he usually did and just get on the city bus instead of going into school. They wouldn't be missed until they were already on their way back, and by then they should have some answers. At least they might know what sort of things were going on back at Sam's house. Kelly looked up and down the hall to re-orient herself, then headed down a corridor she hoped would bring her back to the elevators. She had to start laying the lie if she wanted it to sound believable.

CHAPTER ELEVEN

Wayne was standing near the window, looking down at the street when Kelly rejoined the family in Sam's room. Mom used a napkin to cover over the half of the sandwich she had left sitting on the little rolling bedside table and leaned back in her chair, carrying her coffee with her. She looked up at Kelly, watching as Kelly quickly surveyed the room.

"Dad is talking with the nurse at the desk. He'll be back soon," she said, rightly guessing Kelly's next words and forestalling them.

Kelly nodded. "Ok. Has Sam woken up yet?"

Mom shook her head, but a noise from Sam's bed caused them all to turn and see Sam's eyes fluttering. Kelly stepped around to the side of the bed near the window. Mom stood too quickly and sloshed her coffee over her hand in her haste to sit on the edge of Sam's bed.

"Sam, honey, open your eyes. That's my girl," Mom said.

Sam opened bleary eyes and moved her mouth groggily. After a few moments, she whispered, "thirsty." Mom motioned at Wayne, who poured a paper cup of water from a plastic pitcher on the bedside table and handed it to her. Mom held the cup of water to Sam's mouth and tipped it so that water just touched her lips. She pulled it away after Sam managed a small sip.

"You have to sit up in bed if you want more," she said. "I don't want you to choke on it because you're trying to drink laying down. Do you think you could sit up a bit, honey?"

Sam's eyes had already closed. She shook her head feebly against the pillow. Her breathing settled into a steady pace again as she began to drift back to sleep.

Kelly watched as Mom called Sam's name again and tried to wake her with a few gentle nudges, but Sam was drifting deeper. Kelly tugged at Wayne's arm to get his attention, and the two moved a few steps away from the bed.

"I have a plan, for tomorrow. Just go with it, okay?" She whispered.

Wayne nodded as he watched Mom trying to encourage Sam to wake again. "Kel, you're sure we should," he trailed off as he caught the frown flit across her face.

"Look at her. This isn't normal, no matter what attacked her," she said. "We have to go figure out what happened. We're the only ones who can. If you don't want to go, I'll go by myself. Someone has to do something here, we can't all just sit around." Kelly knew from experience that by goading him the right way, Wayne would do what she wanted. She couldn't leave him behind knowing what she was planning to do, or she risked getting caught earlier than she hoped for.

"No, I'll go. You're right, this isn't normal," he muttered. They turned as a noise from the door behind the curtain drew their attention and Dad walked in.

"Dad, Sam woke up!" Kelly said quickly, drawing his attention to Sam's bed.

He crossed the floor quickly and sat on the other side of the bed from Mom. His hand reached forward and covered Mom's hand on Sam's. Kelly stepped toward the bed and away from Wayne, using Dad's arrival to distract their parents from any suspicions a whispered conversation might generate.

Dad jostled Sam's shoulder to try to get her to wake again. When she didn't open her eyes, he pushed the button for the call light to summon a nurse.

"What was she doing? What did she say?" Dad asked.

"Kelly was just coming into the room and asked if Sam was awake. I said no, but then we heard a noise from her bed. She didn't really say anything, she wasn't awake for more than a couple of seconds," Mom explained. "She said she was thirsty and I gave her a sip of water, but she wouldn't sit up to drink more, she just drifted back into sleep."

A nurse stepped through the curtain. Seeing everyone gathered around Sam's bed, she moved in and began assessing the machines and screens attached to Sam. Mom gave her explanation a second time while the nurse took a small flashlight out and, lifting each of Sam's eyelids one at a time, waved the flashlight near her eyes so that she could watch the pupils contract.

"It's likely that she will still take some time to come fully out of this, but rousing for brief moments like this is normal and to be expected," she said, putting the flashlight back in her pocket. "She had a long surgery, which means a lot of anesthesia, and, as I told you, there was already quite a bit of narcotic in her system. All of that takes time to clear," she directed her comments to Dad. "We're giving her saline, which should help her kidneys flush out more quickly, but since we don't know what she had ingested, we don't know how long it will take for her to come out of this."

Dad nodded, one hand squeezing Mom's shoulder. "Okay, but I thought I understood that you were suggesting that if she started to come out of it soon, it indicates a better prognosis. So, this type of waking up is good news, isn't it?"

"Yes, if it starts now and continues, increasing in frequency as the hours pass, this is good. This is what we expect will happen, to be honest, but not knowing what she already had in her system leaves us blind in suggesting any real timeline. If she was using a prescription drug like oxy, it would mean one thing, but if she was using some street mix, it could mean something completely different. Until she starts having more of these episodes, we won't really know."

Kelly looked at Wayne, willing him to see the need to follow their plan. If Sam had been on drugs, she had to have been taking them where she lived, not on the bus ride home yesterday. She glanced back at Sam's face as her mother glanced around, not wanting to alert her to any undercurrents that might make her suspicious.

The room was quiet as the nurse stepped into the hallway. Finally, Mom spoke.

"So, at the desk, they were telling you that Sam was taking drugs?"

Dad sank down to sit on the edge of the bed. His hand was still on Mom's shoulder, but now he slid it down and grasped her hands with his, Sam's legs sandwiched between them on the bed.

"Yes. They ran some blood tests, some of which have come back. She tested positive for some kind of foreign substance. The tests that would show what she took wouldn't come back for a few more days – they would have to send it to a different lab that is across the state, and they are hoping by then that she will already have come out of this anyway. If she didn't start coming around by tomorrow, they thought they would have to do those tests, but this makes it look like they won't need to do them now."

Kelly looked at Sam's face. Her skin was smooth, unflawed except for the small scar on her chin from when she went over the handlebars on her bike when she was seven.

"Dad, Mom - Sam doesn't do drugs. She wouldn't," she said.

Dad shook his head. "I know, it doesn't sound like Sam, Kelly, but look at the evidence – these blood tests don't lie. She isn't waking up. Her journal posts were becoming increasingly disturbed. I don't like to admit it, but I think we have to accept that Sam was living a life none of us knew about." His shoulders sagged.

Mom drew his head down on her shoulder and held him, resting her head on his. Her hand rubbed his back in small circles. They sat quietly, watching Sam sleep.

CHAPTER TWELVE

K elly gazed, unseeing. She remembered Sam at youth group, telling a group of the girls that their bodies were God's temple – that Christ lived inside their bodies, and that she didn't believe that Christ wanted to get high. Sam wasn't one to say one thing and mean another. If Sam had changed enough to be using drugs, wouldn't it be apparent in other areas of her life, too?

Kelly's attention snapped back to her parents sitting on Sam's bed. Sam's feet, still sandwiched between them, twitched. If Kelly was going to help figure out what had been going on, she needed to get to Sam's apartment tomorrow.

"Rick's parents are moving his stuff out of the dorms," she said into the quiet room.

Her mother turned her head to look at her.

"The zombie party at the student center got a bit out of hand," she said. "A bunch of the kids got arrested for underage drinking, and Rick got a bad cut on his leg and had to have surgery. His parents are really angry, and they're pulling him out of the dorms. He's not sure if they are even going to let him stay enrolled in school."

She strolled over and sat in one of the chairs near the window and looked out at the street. If she didn't appear to attach too much importance to this, it would work.

Mom pursed her lips into a frown. Kelly wasn't sure how she managed to get her mouth to move like that, but it was usually a tell-tale sign that she was annoyed.

"From the sounds of it, I don't think I blame them," Mom said. "How many times has he changed his major? I think he enjoys the partying side of college more than the studying side. Commuting might make him realize what he's there for."

Kelly shrugged one shoulder. She didn't disagree with her mother's assessment, but Rick was a pretty good kid. They'd been friends since middle school. Rick might act like he wanted to take things further, but Kelly thought that was because he didn't pay enough attention to their differences to realize they wouldn't make a good match.

"I know," she said, wanting to keep the conversation going. "This is more than Rick switching majors, though. A lot of the professors are really cracking down because of the party. Rick said the school has started an investigation and the student center has been closed until further notice."

"I guess that doesn't surprise me, either," Mom said. "For the school, there's bound to be liability involved. If any of the under-aged students got hurt, there could be some serious consequences for the school."

Kelly didn't care about the liability any more than she cared about Rick switching majors – less, actually, since Rick really did need to figure out what he was going to do before he graduated. She was slowly reeling the conversation closer to her real objective.

"Well, I want to get to school early tomorrow. If the professors are trying to make sure everyone is walking the line, I want to make sure I've got my assignments done, and I'm ready for class. I know I've got the syllabus, but some of the readings are from texts that I've been borrowing from the library. I didn't think it was worth spending the money for the textbook if we were only going to read a few chapters of the book – even used, the social studies text was over $100."

Dad had picked his head up when Kelly mentioned heading to school. Now he cleared his throat to speak, but Kelly headed him off.

"If Sam is starting to come out of this, which that nurse said is probably what is happening, then it's not really necessary to stay here, is it?" Kelly included both parents in her gaze, imploring them to agree. "It's not that I don't care – I do, but we've already missed one day of school. How far behind do we have to get? I have to work on the weekend, so it's not like I have time to play catch-up."

Kelly could see Mom squeeze Dad's hand laying on the bed. "No, you're right. I don't want you missing any more than you have to."

"Are you forgetting the state we found the house in today? Or the fact that someone cut the brake lines in your car?" Dad sounded tired, but also angry. "The fact remains that someone has targeted this family. I don't think I'm comfortable resuming life as usual just yet."

Kelly's mouth went dry. As ridiculous as it was, she actually had forgotten for a few minutes about the house and her car. As her mind began tossing around for something to say, Wayne spoke up.

"Dad, have the police gotten back to you yet? I know it all seems like it's related, but what if it was a coincidence that someone trashed the yard the same night Sam was attacked? I mean, Sam's attack wasn't related to the party at the college, but that all happened the same time and caused the hospital to have more than they would think normal all on the same night, right?" Wayne threw himself backward in the chair and ran his hands through his hair. "I'm going to be seriously ticked if someone from school did this."

Dad looked at Wayne. His head tipped to one side as he considered Wayne's suggestion. Slowly, he shook his head. "I just don't know. I think it might be a good idea to see what Officer Martin has been able to find out before we make any decisions." He pulled out his phone, took the business card the police officer had given him from his wallet and dialed.

Kelly listened to Dad's side of the conversation breathing a little easier, yet also growing more concerned at the same time. It sounded like the officer agreed with Wayne that it was a coincidence - which would make it easier to convince her parents to let them go to school tomorrow. But it also meant that if the police thought it a coincidence, they wouldn't be looking for more answers - and Kelly knew it couldn't be just coincidence. Someone needed to find out the truth.

She consciously relaxed the muscles in her face, unclenching her jaw and taking a couple of the cleansing breaths her instructor used to urge when Kelly had taken yoga last year. She concentrated on relaxing her shoulders and forearms, releasing the tension so that she could appear calm.

"Well, maybe you're right," Dad said as he flipped his phone shut. "Officer Martin said they still have a few more things to follow up on, but there was another house hit on the other side of town last night. He thinks it more likely that the same group of kids did this than that it was tied to Sam's attack. One of the officers looked at the brake lines of your car, Kelly, and it looks like it was rubbing somehow – it wasn't cut, though there's a definite hole in it. He thought maybe it's been wearing for some time now. You've got triple A, so I guess the smartest thing to do would be to have a tow truck come to take the car to the mechanic and see if any other hoses or lines are going." Dad looked at the phone still in his hand. "I still want you all on your toes. I'm not wholly convinced this is just a prank."

Sam turned her head on the pillow and moved her arm under the covers. Everyone turned to look at her again.

"Officer Martin said he thought it was safe for us to go home," Dad said into the quiet room. "Why don't you two take your mom's car home and make arrangements for your car to be towed, Kelly. You'll have to take the bus to school tomorrow."

Kelly nodded. She stood and walked around the bed to hug her mom. She looked down again at Sam's smooth face as Mom dug through her purse to find the car keys. Sam's eyelashes were long and dark against her pale cheeks. Kelly looked up to see Wayne watching her. As their eyes met, he gave a small nod. Kelly tipped her head almost imperceptibly. They needed to do this for Sam.

CHAPTER THIRTEEN

Kelly found Mom's car in the parking lot by hitting the alarm button on the key fob. She and Wayne wound their way through the maze of other vehicles without speaking. After starting the car, Kelly swung the seat belt across her belly and clicked it in. Wayne was already reaching for the radio buttons. Neither of them wanted to listen to Mom's easy listening station.

"Wonder what other house got TP'd last night," Kelly said, glancing at Wayne as she turned her head to look through the rear window so she could back out of the parking spot. She caught just a hint of a smile cross Wayne's face and stopped the car halfway out of the spot. "What was that? You know something!"

Wayne shrugged his shoulders and tried to look nonchalant, but couldn't stop a grin from splitting his face. "You think you're the only one who knows how to pull something over on their parents?" When Kelly continued to stare at him without moving the car, he continued. "Okay, okay. I called some of the guys from the team. They kind of owe me, don't you think? Only a few of us had to do that street clean-up for the last house - there were a lot more involved than got caught, but none of us ratted. One of them has neighbors who have been working funny shifts, sometimes days, sometimes nights. Turns out that last night they were gone all day and most of the night. The guys did the TP'ing today, but the people hadn't woken up yet or something, so they don't know what time it happened. They called it in to the police saying it happened last night."

Kelly nodded, continuing her turn to look out the window and backing out of the spot. She drove out of the parking lot before speaking.

"So the reality is that someone really is targeting our family like Dad said, but now the police aren't going to be following up on it because they think it was whoever did this other one," she said slowly. When Wayne opened his mouth to interrupt, she shook her head. "But, the other part of this reality is that the police were probably going to say that Sam was using drugs and not follow up on the rest of this because there are drugs involved. If anyone is going to get to the bottom of this, it's going to have to be us. I wish that didn't mean misleading the police, but I don't see where we had a choice."

She glanced at Wayne again. "That was really, really smooth. Scary smooth, how you set that all in play."

Wayne grinned again and settled back into his seat. "Yeah, well, that's how I roll."

At the house, Kelly called the garage to make arrangements for them to fix the brake lines on her car and then called triple A to get a tow truck out to bring it to the garage. Knowing it would take a while before the tow truck got to the house she pulled up the school website and began to look up the syllabus from each class to make sure she had what she needed for each class. She had missed her sociology class today, and public speaking. She knew she had a speech due next week but wasn't sure if there was reading she was supposed to have gotten done for today. Tomorrow she had one of her two art classes and a theatrical makeup class. Kelly was sorry she would be missing that one - they were learning about facial reproduction, and she would love to have more opportunity to work with the plasticene she had made the zombie wounds with. She was wondering if she could ask one of her classmates to video any demonstrations for her so she wouldn't miss out completely when the tow truck driver showed up.

Wayne and Kelly both watched as the driver hooked the cable to the back of Kelly's car. Kelly explained where the vehicle was to be taken, and why she couldn't drive it there. The driver asked her to pop the hood and disappeared under it for a minute. Poking his head around the hood, he motioned for her to join him looking at the engine.

"Something funny about this, to me. I just wanted you to see it before it goes to the shop and any evidence you might need goes away," he said. He pointed to the left side of the engine, where some of the wires had their insulated covering stripped, exposing wires, and the cap to the coolant was missing. Kelly nodded, dampening the growing sense of dread in her stomach. Wayne was looking in the engine with his hands on the fender. He moved a few of the other lines.

"Look, these have rubbed spots too, and there's nothing that could possibly have rubbed against them to cause them. And over there," Wayne pointed to a larger hose toward the middle of the engine, "that one's been rubbed, too. Kelly, you're going to have to have the mechanic go through every line and hose to see whether they're good or need replacing. This is going to take a while, too - and cost some serious cash."

"So who did you guys manage to tick off?" the driver asked, stowing the metal prop and closing the hood of the car while he looked at Wayne's car parked next to Kelly's. The shaving cream had dried on both vehicles to a white film, but Wayne's seats were slashed and ripped apart, and the huge hole where the radio had been was apparent even with the doors closed.

Kelly put her hands up to her temples.

"Just take it, please," she told the driver. "Thank you for showing me. Please take it to the garage, and I'll call to let him know it's more than just the brake lines. I can't - this is just making me sick."

They watched as the driver loaded the car onto his flatbed and headed down the street. Looking at the toilet paper and silly string still strewn about the yard, Kelly sighed.

"C'mon. They'll expect this stuff cleaned up before they get home," she said. She walked to the shrubs in front of the kitchen and started stripping the paper from its leaves.

Wayne headed out to the trees near the street and jumped for a low-hanging piece of paper hanging like a streamer. He managed to pull down quite a bit before the strip broke off, caught by a twig.

"I'm going in to get a trash bag. We're going to need it," he said.

He walked into the house and returned with two bags. Handing one to Kelly, he walked over to the pile of paper he had left and jumped for another low-hanging strip. Kelly moved quickly around the shrubs near the house, restoring them to their un-besmirched state. Reaching past the shrubbery to the windows to peel away the string looped all over them, she realized that she could see directly into her basement studio room.

"Hey, Wayne, do you think that whoever did this followed Sam, or do you think they knew where she was going and were here before her?" She called.

Wayne was working on clearing the mailbox of the silly string. He walked over to where Kelly stood, bag half full of paper and string in his hand.

"Do you think they followed Sam? Or do you think they knew she was coming home and they were here before her," she asked again. She pointed into the window to the room they had been getting ready for the party in when Mom and Dad left the house to get Sam from the bus station. "Because that's really creepy if they were standing here, watching us as we were getting dressed and everything." She shuddered.

Wayne looked through the window, then down at the ground. The mulch had grass growing through it, and silly string had dropped onto the ground under the window. It was impossible to see any footprints.

"I don't know. It doesn't really change anything, does it? Someone has targeted us. They trashed our cars. They assaulted Sam. They trashed the house. Sam's somehow involved with drugs, and we're not going to get to the bottom of anything until we get into her apartment. Whether they were watching us before they hurt Sam or whether they hurt her first and then came to destroy the house, does it make it less creepy?"

No, Kelly thought, it probably didn't make it any less creepy, but somehow it felt it. Thinking that someone had actually stood there in the shadows while she was applying her makeup, fixing her ripped clothes to make sure the wounds showed through, and joking with Wayne about whether to put the spike through his brain or his jaw gave her a chill in the pit of her stomach. Knowing whoever it was had come to the house when they weren't there was one thing, but somehow standing in the bushes made them so much more like a stalker.

"I guess not," she said.

They finished cleaning up the shrubs and lawn quickly, not worrying about the little bits of string left on the grass here and there. Kelly went in to call the garage and explain about the hoses. Listening to the mechanic trying to make space in his calendar intensified the sick sensation in the pit of her stomach. She wouldn't get her car back for at least a week or two, and that was counting on the damage not being too severe. He had agreed to fit the brake line job in tomorrow, but it was going to take a lot more time than he had available tomorrow to go through all of the lines in the car. Kelly agreed to leave the car with him so that he could take a look at it in between other jobs.

"You were right," she told Wayne as he came through the door. "It's going to take a long time for them to go through my car."

Wayne nodded. He threw himself into a chair at the kitchen table and threw his head back to stare toward the ceiling.

"I was trying to figure out how much money it took me to restore that car," he said. "I can't even come close. I mean, I'm not even counting the hours and hours Dad and I put into it, just the money for the seats and parts. The stereo alone was over $500, not including the speakers. I really hope they can figure out who did all this because I want them to pay for the repairs. This just sucks." He was looking at his hands now, picking at a corner of his fingernail.

Kelly sighed. "Then let's hope we can find something at Sam's tomorrow," she said. "Because otherwise, they're not even looking for anyone, remember? They think it was just a prank."

CHAPTER FOURTEEN

"Thanks for dropping me, Dad," Kelly said, opening the car door and stepping out onto the curb. She reached into the back seat to grab her school bag. "Tell Mom to make sure she eats something today."

The bus stop at the corner of the grocery store lot was only a couple of blocks out of Dad's way on the way to the hospital, but Kelly still felt like she was on tenterhooks. She needed Dad to drive away without waiting for the bus to show up. Wayne had already left for school, getting the school bus on the corner of their street. He planned to ride to school and cut across the parking lot instead of going into the building. He was probably already inside the store, waiting for Dad to drive away before coming out to meet her.

"You're sure you're okay with taking the bus home after class?" Dad asked.

"Yeah, I'll either catch the bus or get a ride with someone. I'll be fine," she said. They'd been over this already last night and again this morning, and Kelly had to remind herself to breathe slowly to keep her irritation from showing. "Send a text - I mean, have Mom text, if Sam wakes up. I'll come here instead of home after class, okay?"

She straightened up and stepped away from the car, silently willing him to take the hint and move on. She waved as he lifted his hand and then turned to pull into traffic. She stepped into the bus shelter and watched as he turned the corner a few blocks away and then turned to look toward the store to see if Wayne was coming. Two more minutes ticked by as she waited, growing increasingly frantic as she saw the bus lumbering down the road. She looked up and down the street, back into the store parking lot, and back at the bus. Wayne was nowhere in sight. Kelly took out her phone to text him as the bus pulled up in front of the stop. She flipped her phone case open just as it buzzed to signal an incoming text.

"Already on the bus - got on at the earlier stop."

It was from Wayne. Kelly pushed her phone back into her bag as she mounted the steps to the bus and moved back to sit in the seat next to him at the back of the bus.

"Seriously? You almost gave me a heart attack!" she scolded him.

"I had the time, and we couldn't be sure Dad wouldn't hang around to make sure you got on safely," Wayne said, grinning. "Have you got the money for the tickets? I brought some stuff for lunch in my bag, but I only have $10 on me. We could stop at the bank if we need more to get home with, but my ATM card doesn't work as a debit."

Kelly assured him she had enough money. They needed to change buses at the station, and she did have a debit card. "We're only going to have about six minutes to change buses, though, so we'll have to be quick."

They rode in silence for the rest of the trip to the station. Kelly felt the nervous thrill of anticipation, tinged with something she couldn't quite put a name on. It had something to do with sneaking what they were doing behind her parents' backs, though, and felt a little like shame.

Grabbing their bags, they stood as the bus swayed into the station. They moved quickly down the aisle to the door, past several people just beginning to rise or gather belongings, and reached the sidewalk moments after the bus had come to a complete stop. Kelly looked around the station at the signs hanging just above the milling crowd, scouting the ATM. It was over in the corner near the bathrooms, but there was a line of several people waiting to use it. She shook her head and headed for the ticket counter.

"We'll get round-trip tickets, they're good for any trip and will be easier than trying to get tickets later. Just don't lose it," she said as she stepped into line.

Wayne didn't reply. Kelly turned her head to make sure he was still with her. She couldn't believe the number of people taking the bus this early in the morning. They only had four minutes before their bus was scheduled to take off, they couldn't afford to get separated. Wayne jerked his head at the desk to indicate that the window was open. They moved forward and in less than a minute had two tickets in hand.

Reading the signs overhead again, Kelly and Wayne sprinted toward the fourth bus platform and climbed the stairs to the bus. "You're going to Bridgeville, right?" Kelly asked the driver. At his silent nod, they passed him their tickets, waited until he punched them, and moved back to sit in seats at the back of the bus. Settling into the seat, Kelly pulled out her Theater Makeup textbook and leaned back, preparing to read.

"You brought schoolwork?" Wayne asked, incredulous.

"What?" Kelly looked at him, surprised. "Of course I brought schoolwork. It's a two-and-a-half hour ride, and I have to get this done this week. What else should I do? What are you going to do?"

Wayne shook his head in mock disgust at her. "What any sane person would do. Sleep."

He reclined his chair the few inches it would go, stretched his legs out into the aisle, crossed his arms across his belly, and closed his eyes.

Kelly smirked. "Okay, fine. But when you're pulling D's in class again, you can't blame it on this little adventure." She consulted the syllabus she had clipped to the front page of the textbook and turned to the next assigned reading.

CHAPTER FIFTEEN

The bus lumbered to a stop at a posted bus stop in front of a coffee shop. Kelly and Wayne filed off the bus with their bags slung over shoulders. Wayne had actually managed to fall asleep during the ride, but Kelly hadn't gotten far in her reading. She was too distracted by the people boarding and unboarding in each town on the way. One mother had boarded with a toddler firmly in hand. They sat in the middle of the bus, but the toddler kept turning around to look at the other people on the bus.

"Look, Mommy! A suitcase!" she said, pointing at a businessman's briefcase. A few seconds later she had spotted Wayne's backpack. "Mommy - Backpack! Like Dora's!" Her high-pitched voice sounded like Minnie Mouse to Kelly. The mom seemed very patient with her daughter, though she smiled apologetically to the businessman and threw a quick smile back toward Kelly and Wayne.

Kelly mused whether they were heading to daycare, or whether they were off running errands. Her curiosity was satisfied by one of the mother's whispered comments. "Yes, you can watch Dora when we get to Nana and Papa's house. Can you turn and sit here in the seat next to Mommy, like a big girl?"

The little girl turned and sat, though that request had to be repeated several times before they got off the bus in the next town.

Now, Kelly settled her messenger bag firmly on her shoulder. She knew the way to Sam's apartment, although Sam had borrowed a friend's car to pick her up when she had visited over the summer. It would take longer than she liked to walk there, but it was manageable.

Wayne tugged her sleeve as she took a step down the sidewalk. "Sorry, Kel, I have to grab a coffee first. Come on, it won't take long," he said, tugging her into the coffee shop.

As Wayne stepped up to the counter to order, Kelly browsed the bulletin board near the door. This was no chain restaurant - it had a warm, cozy feel to it. Several patrons sat on stools gathered around small tables on one side of the entry, while the counter and bakery case were on the other side. A man leaned back in an overstuffed chair, a newspaper held open in front of him so that Kelly could not see his face. One hand snuck out to pick up his coffee cup from a small table to the side of the chair. One wall held a high bar with tall stools, upon which sat a few students in front of laptops. Kelly turned back to the counter where Wayne waited for the server to finish making his coffee - he had ordered something with whipped milk and caramel. A red piece of paper tacked to the bulletin board caught her eye. It was advertising guitar lessons in a private home. A business card next to the red paper had a line drawing of a bicycle on it. It was a shop offering bicycle rentals. She reached forward and pulled the card from the board.

"Can you tell me where this shop is?" Kelly held the business card out to the woman behind the counter. Receiving directions to a shop two blocks away, Kelly nodded and thanked her. She pulled out a pen and wrote the address on her palm, then stuck the card back on the bulletin board.

Wayne took his coffee from the teen who had been adding the caramel, smiled at her and tucked a dollar in the tip cup on the counter before turning and nodding at Kelly. "All set?" he asked. He smiled as she rolled her eyes, then held the door open for her to pass through in front of him.

Kelly suggested a detour to see if the bike shop had bicycles to rent for a reasonable price before heading to Sam's apartment. Nodding and sipping his too-hot coffee, Wayne fell into step beside her. The morning was crisp but not cold. The walk to the shop took just minutes. There were bicycles lined up in a bike rack in front of the store, ranging from basic transportation to those specialized for racing and mountain trails. In short time, Kelly and Wayne had each picked out a basic bicycle. Kelly used her bank card to rent the bikes for the day, inwardly grimacing a little at the steep deposit. "That part you get back when you bring the bikes back," the cashier explained. "You know, in the same shape." Kelly declined to rent the helmets the cashier recommended. "I'm not wearing something that's been on 100 other people's heads," she shuddered. "Ick."

Throwing a leg over the back of the bike, Wayne pushed off. Kelly followed suit. She felt a sense of satisfaction, both that she didn't have to walk the three and a half miles to Sam's apartment, and that she had found such a convenient, affordable solution. Problem-solving in the real world, her mom liked to say, takes both a bit of common sense and also a bit of thinking outside the box. Using just one without the other usually turned in less than wonderful solutions. They rode easily, cresting a few hills breathing a little harder than normal but gliding down the far sides to catch their breaths. Pulling up in front of the tenement, Kelly put one foot down on the street and leaned the bike so that she could look around.

The apartment was on the first floor of a three-story building. The neighborhood was scattered with these sort of homes as well as single-family homes, each with a lawn and parking area. Sam's apartment had a flower garden in the front yard and hydrangea bushes under the windows. The hydrangea flower heads had all turned a coppery color now, but Kelly remembered them being blue during the summer. Sam loved tending the flowers - she had helped Mom at home when she was younger, and Kelly knew she had worked out a deal with her landlord that knocked a little off her rent for keeping the gardens presentable.

Looking up and down the street, Kelly couldn't see anyone outside. She and Wayne wheeled the bikes toward the driveway and leaned them against a light post near the end of the walkway leading to the door. Kelly found the key Sam had shown her hidden under one of the flower pots near the patio and unlocked the door of the apartment. She pushed open the door quietly and carefully, motioning for Wayne to be quiet.

"We need to go carefully right from the door, okay? We need to notice everything because we don't know what might be important. In fact," she took out her cell phone and opened the camera app, "I'm going to get photos of everything before we touch anything."

Wayne nodded, glancing around outside. As Kelly snapped a few pictures of the dining area, she moved into the room, making room for Wayne to step inside and close the door.

The dining room was really just a portion of the open floor planned apartment between the living room and kitchen. The square table was pushed against the wall, and three chairs were placed around its sides. The fourth chair sat beside the door holding a small stack of folded blankets. Kelly knew the roommates preferred to keep the thermostat a little low in the cooler months to save on the heating bill. She recognized two of the blankets as throws Sam had taken from home.

The kitchen was to the right of the dining room. It was small, but large enough for a couple of college students who didn't do a lot of big home-made meals. It was u-shaped, with the kitchen sink along the far wall underneath a window that looked out over the hydrangea bushes. During the summer, Kelly had been able to smell the flowers through the open window as she washed the dishes. The stove was on the wall shared by the bathroom, with the refrigerator on the wall that faced the front porch. A short hallway on the wall between the kitchen dining area led to the bathroom and the two girls' bedrooms.

The living room area was on the other side of the room. A couch sat with it's back toward the dining area, it's upholstery sporting large yellow flowers on a cream background. A low coffee table was in front of the couch. A pair of wing-backed chairs sat on the other side

of the room, flanking a window that looked out over a short picket fence and into the neighbor's driveway. A small end table sat between the two chairs, supporting a stack of books and a pile of index-
sized note cards. Kelly recognized one of the books in the stack as
one that Sam had brought home on her last visit at the beginning of
school. An old cabinet TV set sat on the floor in front of a large picture window that looked out on the porch. Kelly knew that most of
the furniture had come with the apartment and had likely been cast
off decades earlier, but aside from looking dated, the apartment had
a warm feeling about it.

She snapped a few more pictures as they moved into the room,
making sure to get close-ups of the items on the table, the few dishes
left in the dish drainer on the counter, and the message board on the
wall near the telephone in the kitchen. She opened the fridge and
snapped a photo of the contents, a small frown hovering over her lips
as she did so.

"Wayne, look at this," she said. She wasn't surprised, after reading
the posts in Sam's journal, but it was still unsettling to see the empti-
ness of the refrigerator.

Wayne came up behind her and peeked over her shoulder. He
pointed at a take-out container on the bottom shelf. "That's not
right. Take more pictures," he said, pulling the styrofoam box out of
the fridge and putting it onto the counter. Written on the top of the
container in ballpoint pen were the letters "MK."

Kelly hadn't even noticed them. She took a photo of the box
with the cover on, and Wayne flipped the container open. Inside was
half of a pita-roll sandwich, lettuce, chicken, and shredded cheese
spilling out from the cut end. Wayne picked up a piece of the shredded lettuce and put it in his mouth.

"Still kind of crunchy," he said. "Which means it can't be that
old. Definitely not three or four days old, which it would have to be
if it was here when Sam freaked and headed home."

Kelly and Wayne stared at each other. Kelly looked around the house again, listening intently. She couldn't hear anything other than an occasional vehicle passing on the street out front. Holding her finger to her lips, she moved quietly toward the bedroom doors.

CHAPTER SIXTEEN

G rabbing the door handle of Sam's bedroom door, Kelly turned it slowly and quietly. She eased the door open a few inches and peeked inside, then opened it more. There was no one in Sam's room. They turned to look at the other bedroom door. Wayne grabbed the knob and quietly opened that door, mimicking Kelly's movements of minutes before.

There was no one in that room, either, but that was where the similarities between the two rooms ended. Where Sam's room was neat and orderly, much like the rest of the apartment, Jill's room looked like her dirty hamper had been tossed all over the place. A couple of used glasses sat on the top of the dresser, along with some crumpled napkins, an apple core, several books, a shoe, and a jewelry box, as well as a shallow dish filled with earrings that hadn't made it back into the jewelry box. The bed was unmade and missing a bottom sheet entirely. A waste paper basket near the bed was overflowing with crumpled paper and old take-out Styrofoam coffee cups. A shelf in front of the window was covered with several bumpy, spiky cactus and two rows of pill bottles. The room had a stale odor of old food and dirty clothes, mixed with something else that Kelly couldn't put a name to but found equally unpleasant.

"Whoa," said Wayne. "Who knew Jill was such a pig?"

Kelly shook her head, putting her finger to her lips quickly. There was still the bathroom to check to see if someone was in the apartment. She moved quickly and quietly to the final door in the hall and repeated the slow, quiet knob turn. The bathroom was empty, but Kelly was positive it had been used that morning. The lid to the toilet was up. A dirty hand towel was tossed carelessly on the edge of the vanity. A bath towel had been dropped and left on the floor in a crumpled heap, and a small puddle still on the floor was evidence that someone had stepped out of the shower onto the tile floor without using a bath mat.

"Someone was definitely here this morning, for the water to still be on the floor," she said, taking photos of the room. "Dad said Sam thinks Jill was killed - so either Jill was here and left this mess, and Sam was wrong, or Sam was right, and someone else has been staying in the apartment while Sam's been in a hospital two hours away."

"Kelly! Oh my word, you have to come see this!" Wayne said. He motioned frantically for Kelly to follow him back into the smelly room and walked over to the closet door. "I was wondering what she was keeping in the closet since so many of her clothes are all over the floor. Either she was using the closet for something else, or she has more clothes than you and Sam combined."

He threw open the closet door, flipping the light switch on the wall as he did so. He pointed at a couple of cardboard boxes that said they held computer paper. "Who needs reams of computer paper? Hurry up and take some photos, OK? We definitely don't want to hang around here too long."

Kelly reached a hand forward, lifted the lid of the top box and gasped, fumbling the cover and dropping it. "Oh my God, are those hands? Wayne, those are hands!" She picked up the lid again, revealing the contents of the box. Inside were several sealed plastic bags of what certainly looked like mummified hands, as well as similar bags with what looked like dried brown balls of skin.

Kelly raised her phone again and snapped a couple of photos before carefully replacing the lid. They shut the light off and closed the closet door, careful to make sure it didn't look as though anything had been disturbed. Stepping backward, Kelly decided they'd better take a peek through the rest of the room before leaving. She turned to the dresser and opened each drawer, snapping a photo of the contents before touching anything. In the topmost drawer, she found a carton of plastic bags used to package jewelry in next to a digital scale. Aside from unfolded clothes and a drawer full of half-empty liquor bottles, she found nothing remarkable in the rest of the dresser. She took photos of the shelf in front of the window, with a close up of the label-less pill bottles. Kelly hesitated, then took the lids off the two front bottles on the shelf, took photos of the pills inside, and replaced the covers, trying to put the bottles back precisely where they had been.

The drawer of the bedside table held an assortment of old pens, a phone charger, a maroon notebook with a pen tucked inside that Jill had apparently been using as a journal, and a framed photo of Jill and Sam, taken their first year as roommates at the college dorm. Kelly hesitated a fraction of a second before grabbing the notebook and closing the drawer. She stuffed the notebook into the messenger bag still slung over her shoulder.

"I don't know - it might give us nothing, but you're right, I don't want to hang around here too long, and maybe there is something in there that will explain, well, some of this, at least," she said in response to Wayne's raised eyebrow.

Wayne nodded, then walked to the door of the room. "Can we please get going? Seriously, Kel, we need to not be here."

Kelly followed him out, turning to look over the room again before closing the door. She performed the same routine in Sam's bedroom, taking photos of every drawer, but found nothing unusual. Sam was neat, liked her things just so, and kept her closets and drawers tidy and organized. It had been brutal for Kelly to share a room with her when they were younger.

Wayne had gone back into the main room. "Kelly! Kelly!" His insistent whisper was just loud enough for her to hear.

Darting to the door of Sam's bedroom, Kelly saw Wayne flattened against the wall, peeking out the window. He glanced at her quickly before turning his attention back to the window.

"Someone just pulled up out front," he whispered. "It's a guy. He's messing with the trunk. Kelly, what are we going to do?"

Kelly reached over quickly and pulled the bathroom door closed. "Lock the door, Wayne," she hissed at him. "It was locked when we got here. Where's your bag?"

Wayne's hands trembled as he turned the lock in the center of the doorknob, trying not to make noise. He grabbed his bag, which he had dropped inside the door when they first came in. He half-walked, half-slunk behind the couch, trying to stay out of view from the window. He reached Kelly's side and the two slipped back into Sam's room and closed the bedroom door.

"Should we hide in her closet?" Wayne asked. "Just in case he checks in here?"

Kelly nodded. She had been thinking the same thing. Suddenly, though, she held clenched hands to her forehead. "Wayne, the bikes! We left them leaning against the lamp post! He'll see them!"

Wayne stared at her, then looked wildly around the room. "The window!"

Trying to move as quietly as possible, they crossed the room to assess the possibility. The window faced the same neighbor's drive-way that the window between the chairs in the living room faced. There were no vehicles in the driveway.

"If we can get out and get on the other side of that house, we can watch and wait for him to leave," Wayne suggested, moving to un-lock the window.

Kelly groaned quietly but nodded. He hung his backpack out the window and dropped it softly on the ground beneath them. As he swung his legs out the window, he pointed with his hand toward the rear corner of the house. "We have to make sure we go that way, so he doesn't see us from the living room window." He dropped down to join his backpack.

Kelly turned her head to listen for the front door, but heard nothing. She swung one leg out the window and pulled the second out. She was getting ready to jump when she heard the key being turned in the lock on the front door. She bent to get her head through the window and pushed against the wall with her feet to clear the window. The impact sent her sprawling. Wayne pulled her quickly to her feet. Keeping close to the side of the house, they worked their way quickly to the back corner of the house. The neighbor's picket fence was too high to jump, and not sturdy enough to try to climb over, but it only went the length of the yard. Glancing again at the window they had climbed out of, Kelly pointed at the back corner of the fence. They ran, making the end and ducking behind the fence quickly. Wayne snuck glances around the side of the fence for a few minutes until they were sure they hadn't been seen.

CHAPTER SEVENTEEN

"We didn't close the window," Kelly moaned, sneaking a glance at the building between the slats of the picket fence. "What if he opens the door to Sam's room? What if a breeze comes up and he realizes there's a window open somewhere and starts looking?"

She turned her face from the apartment building and looked back at the house on this side of the fence. A cat sitting on the table on the back deck looked at them with idle curiosity. Kelly closed her eyes, hoping they didn't also have a dog somewhere on the property.

Wayne was still peering around the fence at the apartment. "He hasn't noticed anything yet," he said, "or, at least he hasn't stuck his head out the window yet. There's no breeze to come up, and it's a little cool out here, but Sam likes to keep her apartment cool, so maybe he won't notice that, either."

He turned back to Kelly and took a deep breath, blowing it out slowly. "That was quick thinking, about the lock," he said. "You're a little scary, how fast your brain works."

Kelly opened her eyes and gave a weak smile. "Yeah, well, that's how I roll," she said. Glancing around the yard again, and back at the apartment with the window wide open, she pointed to the other side of the deck. "Do you think we should try to make it to there? If he does look out that window, we're probably too easy to spot sitting here."

Wayne looked at the deck, then around at the yard around them, considering.

"There isn't a lot of cover in this yard, besides this fence," he said. He jerked his thumb at the blockade fence separating the back property line from the next yard. "And this pretty much keeps us out of any of the yards on that street back there. Do you want to try -" but what he was going to suggest was lost as they heard the screen door on the porch of Sam's apartment swing on its hinges.

Both ducked lower and tried to take up as little room as possible on the ground. Kelly had her head against the fence and risked a searching sweep of her eyes to see if the man was heading toward them. She held her breath as the sound of his steps tapped down the steps and strode briskly to the car. They listened as he opened the door, and slid into the driver's seat. The engine hummed a few times before catching, then the car was thrown into reverse and roared out of the driveway. Another few seconds passed with the sound of the vehicle fading away as it drove down the road while Kelly and Wayne stayed frozen where they were.

Slowly, Kelly lifted her head and turned to Wayne. He sat back heavily and leaned against the fence.

"How did we manage that?" he asked softly. He wiped the palms of his hands on his legs.

Kelly shook her head. Her heart was still beating to burst out of her chest. She put one shaking hand up to pull a strand of hair away from her face and tucked it behind her ear. "Do you think we need anything else inside the apartment? Or do you think we have enough?" She waited half a beat before adding, "Because, to be honest, I think I'd rather grab the bikes and go back to town. We can sit in the coffee shop and look through what we've got. Or we can go to a park - there's one Sam used to take me to, where she used to go jogging. It's not too far from here. No one would think to look for us there."

Wayne nodded. "The park would be better than the coffee shop, I think," he said. "Not as many ears to overhear so we don't have to be so careful about what we say." He stood. "Let's just close the window first. We can do it from outside - at least get it mostly closed, anyway. That way if he didn't see it just now, it'll buy us more time before he does."

Kelly nodded but didn't move. She was willing her heart to stop pounding so hard. Her hands clenched the grass as though to secure her body to the ground.

"Just, let's sit here just a couple of minutes, OK? Just a couple," she said, leaning her head back against the fence with her eyes closed.

Wayne peeked back around the fence again. "Kelly, I want to get away from here. We don't know who that was, why he came back, where he just went or when he's coming back again - but we do know there's a couple of boxes of body parts in there, and I don't want to be caught anywhere near that."

Kelly heaved a deep sigh, then nodded slowly as she moved to get to her feet. "Yeah, okay. Let's close the window and get the bikes out of here."

They crossed the backyard to the side of the house and were soon standing under Sam's window. If Kelly reached her hands above her head, she could touch the bottom window sill. Though taller, Wayne couldn't reach the raised window, either. He leaned down and laced his fingers together. Kelly put one foot into his make-shift stirrup, and between the two of them, she managed to grab the window bottom and close the window. She noted the bedroom door, still shut.

They walked cautiously around the back of the building. The car was gone, and no one stood waiting to catch them as they hurried to the bikes they had leaned against the lamp post at the end of the walkway. Wayne slung his backpack over one shoulder, threw his leg over the seat and prepared to ride. Kelly, who hadn't taken her bag off since they had arrived, quickly hopped onto her bike and pushed off. She didn't want to be near the house any longer than they needed to.

She headed down the road, reviewing the route to the park in her mind. Sam had used the trails at the park to run - she had said being in the woods and getting to appreciate nature while also getting her runner's high was the closest to being in Heaven she could imagine.

There were also fields used for team sports and a route set up for doing calisthenics, as well as a playground. When Sam had taken Kelly to the park over the summer, Kelly had walked a few of the wooded trails with her camera while Sam had run. Kelly had some of the photos from that week on her computer at home.

"Hey, Kel - stay up on the sidewalk, okay?" Wayne's voice drifted up to her. "It'd be better to look like we're just out for a ride if that guy comes back - we're headed the same way the car went."

Kelly lifted her head and glanced around, surprised. So lost in remembering, she hadn't realized that Wayne was right. She directed the tires up onto the sidewalk at the next driveway and slowed so that Wayne could pull up alongside her.

Kelly scanned the road ahead. There were a couple of intersections close together; she hoped she could remember which one led to the park. She had been to the park a couple of times with Sam, but each time Sam had been driving, and Kelly had been chattering away, not really paying attention to the directions.

They neared the first intersection. Kelly slowed, looking down the road to the right. Nothing there really looked familiar. Shaking her head, she kept leading toward the next street. At the next right, she looked down the road and was relieved to see a street sign with a picture of a tractor on it. She remembered Sam laughing as she told Kelly about the time she had seen a tractor in line at the coffee shop drive-through when they passed the sign. She took the right and looked for more familiar sights to make sure she was correct. If she was, the park should be coming up in a few minutes.

They rounded a corner in the road. Kelly was struck by how pretty it was in this town, with the Autumn leaves changing color and beginning their drift to cover the edges of the roads and yards. There weren't too many houses on this street; it was mostly wooded with an edging of grass on the side of the street. Ahead, Kelly saw the entrance to the park.

They slowed as they entered the driveway. Kelly noted a few cars in the parking lot. A couple of women were walking around the ball fields with baby strollers. The sound of a ball being hit back and forth drew their attention to the tennis courts, where a couple were in fierce competition. There were fewer people, overall, than when Kelly had been to the park last, but Kelly realized that there would have been more then, as it had been summertime. The park had been alive with screams and laughter from running children. Now, it was a Tuesday, mid-school week, and the majority of those children would be in school.

They walked their bikes over to a picnic table between the ball field and the wooded trails that Sam had used for cross-country running. Kelly sat on the bench with her back to the table and closed her eyes. It would feel nice to sit and relax - if she could pretend that nothing was upside down in her world.

CHAPTER EIGHTEEN

"Ok, so what do we have?" Wayne's words intruded on her fantasy. He sat on the bench beside her.

Kelly opened her eyes and sighed. She dug out a notebook and pen from her messenger bag. Lists always seemed to help her keep her mind organized.

"Well, there's boxes of body parts in Jill's closet! We have a scale and baggies in the drawer in her room, and those weird cacti and bottles of pills on the shelf. We have a man who has obviously been living in Sam and Jill's apartment," she wrote.

"Hang on, we don't know for sure he has been living there," Wayne said. He was rummaging in his backpack.

"He took a shower there! He has a key!" Kelly was irritated.

"Yeah, he had a key," Wayne said. He surfaced from his backpack and looked at her. "Kelly, you've taken showers at other people's houses before and not been living there. Besides, we don't know for sure it was him that took the shower – we just know a shower was taken."

Kelly grimaced. Of course, Wayne was right – his points were entirely logical. Somehow, though, she knew that she was right. She looked at her list and frowned.

"Fine. You make good points. I still think he is living there, though," she said as she scratched out the line that said "man living at Sam's" and wrote instead, "man has key to Sam's," and "someone took shower this morning."

Wayne looked over at the list. His hands were busy pulling sandwiches and juice pouches out of his backpack.

"Don't forget the take-out container," he said, "and the otherwise empty fridge."

Kelly nodded, adding them to the list.

"It's obvious that something was going on," Kelly said. "This isn't all just Sam's imagination."

Wayne had made a stack of food for Kelly and was opening up his own sandwich bag.

"Unless Sam was in on it," he said. Glancing up at Kelly and noticing her glare, he shrugged. "I'm just trying to look at all angles. Isn't that what you said we had to do? Although," he took a bite from his ham and cheese, "it doesn't really look like that. Make another list – we should really make two more. One that lines up stuff that could make it look like Sam was involved, and one of stuff that makes it look like she wasn't involved."

Kelly flipped to a new page in the notebook without speaking. She hated to admit that Wayne was being more logical about this than she was, but she and Sam had been closer that Wayne had been with Sam. Wayne would be happy to have someone else in the family divert the scrutiny off of him.

"Ok, so what makes Sam look like she could be involved?" she asked, prepared to write whatever points he might come up with.

"Well, for starters, she lived in a house that has pills, a scale, baggies, and freaking boxes of body parts in it. C'mon, Kel, Sam isn't stupid. She must have known that stuff was in there," he said.

Kelly didn't answer him but wrote it down. "What else?" she asked.

Wayne shook his head, his mouth full of sandwich. "I don't know," he finally admitted after swallowing the mouthful.

"Ok, so what makes it look like she wasn't involved?" Kelly asked. She started writing. "She was attacked. She is in the hospital. She posted in her journal that things were freaking her out; stuff was being moved, food was tasting funny. At the apartment, everything in the shared spaces – the kitchen and living room – were spic and span and organized, like Sam's room. The only room that was a pig stye was Jill's room – and that door was closed. Sam would have wanted to give Jill privacy, so she wouldn't have gone into her bedroom, would she?"

Wayne had finished his sandwich and started on his apple. "Oh, here's another point for the other list – she had drugs in her system. That's huge, Kel."

Kelly's mouth tightened as she conquered the urge to scream. She added the point to the list.

"Kelly," Wayne's voice was soothing. "I don't want Sam to be involved. I don't. I just want to make sure we are looking at all the angles because, in case you hadn't noticed, we're sitting out here in a park, two and a half hours from home, because we just got chased out of the window of the apartment by someone coming in who shouldn't be there. You said we need to be smart about this, right? So let's be smart. Eat something for lunch."

He nudged the pile of food next to her notebook.

Kelly slapped the pen down on the notebook. "Wayne, honestly! I haven't forgotten we had to jump out of the window. I haven't forgotten how serious this is. I just don't agree that Sam could be involved. I was here over the summer, remember? I know how Sam is – she would not be involved with drugs. I can't even imagine who would be involved with the rest of that stuff!"

She stood up from the bench and started pacing, unable to contain the energy she felt coursing through her body.

"When I was here over the summer, Jill had lost weight. Remember when we saw her at spring break, she was wearing mostly yoga pants and baggie sweatshirts? Sam told me that she had thought Jill might be pregnant – Jill was sick a lot, and she was crying, but she wouldn't tell Sam what was wrong. Then she broke up with her boyfriend. By the end of the school year, she was going with a new guy, but Sam didn't seem to like him. You know Sam, she doesn't really say anything outright bad about anyone, but she just acted like she didn't seem comfortable with him. And Jill changed – and I know, that happens when people start going out with someone, they want to spend all sorts of time together and don't have time for other people anymore. This went beyond that. When I was here in the summer, Jill would write her name on food in the fridge. They never bothered with that before – if Sam wanted a yogurt and didn't have any in there, she'd eat one of Jill's and replace it later."

The more Kelly talked about what had seemed odd over the summer, the more she remembered, and the stranger it seemed.

Kelly stopped pacing and sat on the bench again. She picked up the apple Wayne had packed for her and took a bite absentmindedly, still thinking.

"You remember when Sam came home right before school? She said Jill's boyfriend really made her uncomfortable. She was wondering whether she was going to stick out the lease on the apartment or whether she and Jill would end up splitting and one take the apartment and one leave, because the boyfriend was always there. She said it wasn't anything she could put her finger on, she just didn't care for him." Kelly swallowed the bite of apple. "He wasn't hanging around when I was there at the beginning of summer. I saw him once, but that was when Jill had just started seeing him. They were going to some party at his friends' house, I think. Jill was wearing a really short skirt and had straightened her hair - she looked really different."

"Okay, so she was acting different," Wayne said. He had watched her pace without interruption, but couldn't contain himself anymore. "And Sam probably would have not wanted to go into her bedroom." He stressed the word probably, putting a question into the word. "Kel, maybe we need to start with figuring out where Jill is. Any idea on how to do that?"

Kelly took another bite of the apple and stared into the woods, thinking as she chewed. Jill and Sam had attended a lot of the same classes to begin with, but Sam had branched off into history whereas

Jill had gone into sociology. If they could figure out some of the classes Jill should be taking this semester, they might be able to go to the school and see if she was still attending them. Or, maybe find some other classmates who might be able to give them some insight. Kelly expressed as much to Wayne, surprised when he looked hesitant.

"Do you have a better idea?" she asked, at a loss.

"How are we going to figure out what classes she was in? You know I have a hard time coming up with stories on the fly, Kelly. What if someone asks me something? I don't want to blow it," he said.

Kelly pulled out her phone. "I've got an idea about the classes. What if some of the textbooks were Jill's? Or what if there were some in her room? I took photos of everything in the apartment - we can look through them to see if we see any textbooks. When we get to the school, we can ask at the library what classes are using those text-books - they ought to have copies of all of the textbooks the school is using, in the reference section."

Wayne still looked uncomfortable but nodded. They put their heads together over Kelly's phone as she pulled up the pictures. She skipped to the photos of Jill's room first. She paused at the pictures of the closet, struck anew by the enormity of what they had discovered. She swiped the screen to reveal a photo of the room that included the bed. There was a stack of books on the floor near the bed. Kelly zoomed in, and they were able to see that two looked like textbooks, but Kelly's hand must have been shaking when she took the photo, because the titles of the books were impossible to read, even blown up on the screen.

"Well. We can see if the library has the textbooks where we can see them - we know we're looking for one with a part blue, part or-ange spine, with either white or tan letters. The other one is either White or yellow with green letters, and a blue stripe at the bottom," Kelly said. She swiped the screen again to see if another, clearer picture might have the books, too. The next photo was of the contents of the drawer of the bedside table. "Wait - I took that!" she yelped, putting her phone on the table and reaching into her bag. She pulled out Jill's notebook.

CHAPTER NINETEEN

Putting the notebook on the table, she opened the cover. She had been right, Jill had used the notebook as a journal. It didn't look like she had a regular habit of writing things down, but had used the notebook sporadically. The first few pages were from the beginning of the year. She had still been dating the boy that Kelly's family had all met - Roger. Apparently, Roger was thinking of going to California to law school at the end of the school year, which devastated Jill. Kelly skimmed the pages quickly, gasping when she reached a date in March. Sam had guessed correctly - Jill had been pregnant. The next few pages were full of smudged entries where tears had hit the paper. Roger had given Jill money and taken her to a clinic but hadn't gone inside with her. Kelly felt the licks of white-hot anger in her stomach as she turned the page.

The next entry was dated a few weeks later. There were no more tear stains on the page, but the words felt wooden and stark to Kelly. There were a few entries over the course of a month, each only a couple of sentences long.

Wayne was gazing into the woods as Kelly read. She skimmed the next couple of pages and then came to the first mention of Mark.

"Listen," Kelly read the entry out loud to Wayne. "Met a guy today. Said he's been watching me, and can see the life draining out of my soul. The way he talked was so compassionate. He didn't ask why I am sad or try to get me to laugh. He said he would like me to give him a chance. I asked a chance for what, and he touched my hand, so soft and carefully, and said a chance to help me live. Agreed to go to dinner."

Wayne made a gagging sound in the back of his throat. "Seriously, who would fall for that? Smarmy!"

Kelly looked at him thoughtfully. "Think about it," she said quietly. "She aborted her baby. She was sinking deeper and deeper into depression with every day that went by. She didn't feel comfortable talking to anyone about it, or else Sam would have known. She must have felt alone, like she was drowning, and someone she doesn't even know tells her he can see her." She looked back at the entry. "I do agree, definitely smarmy, but I can understand why she felt drawn to the hope he offered."

She skimmed another few pages. There were several more entries about Mark, and alarms in Kelly's mind were ringing more insistently with each entry. With the comments Jill included that Mark had said, it seemed to Kelly that he had been stalking Jill. Jill appeared to find it romantic. An entry after dinner at a pub one night included news that Mark had started an argument with another man at the bar for bumping into Jill. Jill saw it as protective. Kelly snorted - possessiveness was easy enough to see when it was laid out on the page like this.

"Hey! This one is from the week I visited Sam," Kelly said, outraged at the entry. "She wasn't as nice as she seemed to be! She says here that she is getting tired of Sam's talk about church and Sam's family's talk about church - we didn't even talk to her about church! What a mealworm!"

Kelly continued to skim the entries, noting a subtle change over the next few pages. Mark gave Jill a pill when she said she had a headache, admitting it wasn't aspirin but telling her it would help. Jill described a warm and protective shell surrounding her, keeping pain and badness away. She started having headaches a couple of times a week, or at least, according to her entries, she started telling Mark she had them a couple of times a week. Midway through the notebook, Kelly could see that Jill was using on a regular basis. She never named the actual drug, and Kelly wasn't sure she actually knew what she was taking. She described little pink pills, and a couple of times noted that the pills were blue or green.

"I don't get it," Kelly said, after nearly 10 minutes of reading in silence. "Mark was supplying her with drugs - she doesn't say what kind, but it looks like there were three or four kinds of pills she was taking. But then he would make her get cleaned up and go to class. She said it was important to him to have people think she was good. At one point it seems like she must have asked him about something harder, but he must have said no, because she seems mad at him and about him needing people to see her as good. She talks about some of his friends but says he won't bring her out much and when she runs into any of his friends without him around, they all act like they don't know her, like she's invisible. Which, apparently, she is supposed to do, too. It all seems very bizarre to me, to be honest, Wayne."

Kelly looked up at Wayne. He had turned to sit with his back to her and was tossing twigs at a little pine needle tepee he had set up at the end of the table. "What on earth are you doing?"

"Waiting for you to finish so we can get out of here," he said, calmly. "Remember you said we need to catch the 5:45 bus to get home? It's already almost one."

Kelly jumped. She glanced at her watch and grabbed the notebook and her phone, stuffing them back into the messenger bag. Some folded pages had slipped out of the notebook and fallen onto the table - she shoved those in with the book. She realized that she had eaten the sandwich and finished the apple while reading the journal entries. "You're right - let's go," she said.

Wayne paused as they grabbed the bikes. "Do you know how to get to the school from here, or do we have to go back past Sam's apartment?"

Kelly shook her head.

"No, but at least we can put the name of the school into the GPS," Kelly said. "Better use yours, though - my battery is already half gone."

Wayne nodded, pulled out his phone and tapped in the name of the school. Hitting a couple of tabs, he noted that it would take them almost half an hour to get to the school on bike. Kelly threw her leg over the seat and pushed off, following Wayne out of the parking lot. She was thankful that they turned left out of the park and not right - she really had no desire to go back past Sam's apartment and chance another encounter with the man they had run from. Thinking of that, she hollered ahead to Wayne.

"Hey, that guy at the apartment! I don't think that was Mark," she said when he had slowed enough for her to ride up alongside him. "Mark had to have been slick, right? To draw Jill into his web, and from what I remember he was not bad looking." She tried to remember what he had looked like from the few minutes she had seen him when he was picking Jill up for the party. "The guy at the apartment was kind of scruffy, wasn't he?"

Wayne nodded. The voice on his phone called out directions to take a left in 1000 feet. Kelly couldn't even see a left to take until they rounded a corner.

"Crap!" Wayne's tense whisper came at the same time Kelly saw the car at the intersection. It took a right onto their road and drove past them. The driver was fiddling with the radio. He glanced at them as they rode toward the intersection, then back at the dashboard. Kelly forced herself to keep pedaling and face forward, though her breath caught in her chest. It was the guy from the apartment. Next to her, Wayne had turned to look at the car in the pretense of checking the road behind them in order to take the left turn.

"Oh, man, Kelly, that was way too close!" he whispered as they took the turn and drove on. "I don't know that this is a very good idea."

Kelly secretly wondered about the plan, too. However, remembering Sam's white face on the pillow at the hospital steeled her nerve.

"Wayne - we know that there is a whole crapload of stuff going on. We are the only ones looking for anything more than Sam getting mugged at a bus stop after using drugs. We have to do this! Who else is going to help her?" she said.

"Hey, I want to help Sam, too, but who's going to help us if we end up like she did?" Wayne uttered tersely. They kept pedaling, with increased energy sparked by their fear.

"We're going to be in public once we get to the school," Kelly said. She wasn't sure if she was trying to soothe Wayne's fears or her own, but it helped her feel a little more controlled. "And he didn't see us or know us if he did see us. The car kept going, right? Nobody knows we are here, Wayne. Nobody is going to be looking to hurt us."

Wayne's GPS chirped out directions to take the next right, then find the school on the next street on the right. They had made better time than the half-hour initially forecast - probably because of trying to put as much distance between them and the car as they could.

"Hey, we aren't going to have a long time to stay at the school, either," Wayne commented. "Remember we have to get the bikes back to the shop before they close - that's at 5. Otherwise, you won't get the deposit back. Just keep it in mind that we need to leave enough time to ride back to get there before they close."

Kelly nodded. Wayne had a thing for time, some inner clockwork he ran by, making sure he wasn't late. She was used to him keeping her on track.

They turned in at the first entrance for the school. There was a cut out with a map of the campus, which they used to locate the library on. Pulling back into the main drive, Wayne's front tire hit the grate on a drain cover and twisted, sending him sprawling on the ground. He jumped up quickly, grabbing the bike handles and pulling the bike toward him, but the tire had popped. Grimacing, he pulled the bike to the side of the road. He rubbed his hands on his jeans, leaving a line of blood behind on one leg.

"Jeez, Wayne, are you okay?" Kelly straddled her bike and pulled his hands out to look at them. The asphalt had ripped the palms a little, but she doubted they hurt more than his pride.

"I'm fine," he said, pulling his hands away from her. "Just sting a little. What are we going to do about the tire?"

Kelly looked around. At each building entrance, there were bike racks, most of which had at least a few bikes chained to them. "We can check the bookstore - with this many bikes on campus, they might stock bike supplies," she said.

Wayne nodded, breathing out in disgust. "I'll go there and see, and meet you at the library. If they don't have tubes, you won't have much time to check anything."

Wayne checked the campus map quickly before heading off toward the store, wheeling the bike beside him. Kelly glanced at the map again to refresh her memory and headed to the library, carefully maneuvering around the drainage grate.

CHAPTER TWENTY

Opening the large wooden doors, Kelly took a deep breath. She loved the smell of libraries, the pages and glue used to bind the books, and the quiet scratching of pens on paper and tapping of fingers on keyboards. She quickly located the reference desk and headed over to it, phone in hand. She had decided on a cover story in case she was asked, but there was no one standing at the desk just now. She pulled up the photo of the textbooks to remember what was on the spines and started looking at the books on the shelf behind the desk. She saw one spine with blue and orange, but it was a French text. A white spine with blue lettering looked promising, but it had no blue stripe at the bottom. She kept looking.

"May I help you?" The voice came from behind her left elbow.

Kelly jumped, sliding her phone toward her chest to hide the screen. She turned to see a grey-haired man limping toward her. He wore a sweater with patches on the elbows over a brown plaid flannel shirt that made Kelly wonder how he wasn't melting in a puddle of sweat.

"I'm looking for a textbook," she said. "I can't remember the name of it. It's blue and orange on the spine."

The man pulled glasses from his pocket and put them on his nose as he went around the desk. He pulled a list from beneath the counter. "What class is it for?" he asked, prepared to scan the list.

"I'm not sure," Kelly said. "My sister asked me to see if you have a copy because hers is missing a few pages - I think she bought it used. I can't remember the name or the class, just that it was blue and orange."

The man looked at her over the top of his glasses as he slid the list back under the counter.

"Well, these are the textbooks we have. We don't allow them to leave the library, though," he said. He waved his hand at the shelf behind him. "If we allowed these books to leave, they wouldn't be here for others to borrow."

"No, I know that," Kelly assured him. "My sister knows she'll have to come here to read the pages if you have the book, she just asked me to look since I was going to be here anyway."

The man nodded. He turned to look at the shelf, scanning the spines. Kelly had already ruled out the books on the bottom shelf and was working her way up the wall. She snuck a look at the photo on her phone again. She needed to find a book with either white or tan letters, with a blue and orange spine. The old man pulled out a couple of textbooks with blue or orange on their spines, but neither was the right one. Kelly kept scanning. On the third shelf up, her heart leaped. There was a book with the right colors on the spine, though it had yellow letters in the title. She pointed to the book and asked him to bring it to her to look at.

Looking down at the title, The Sociology of Organizations, Kelly felt a flutter of excitement. She must be on the right track! She had been afraid that it might be a math book or one from some other basic core course that she couldn't be positive about, but Jill was a sociology major. "Um, I think this is the one, but can you tell me which professors are using this textbook?" She asked the librarian.

He pulled his list out from under the counter again. "That's Professor Harlin's text, his class is the only one using it."

Thanking the man for his help, Kelly walked away to a table and sat down. She pulled out the notebook she and Wayne had been making the lists in and wrote down the name of the book and the class. Somehow, she had to figure out how to find some of the other students from the course.

"Hey, aren't you Sam's sister?"

Kelly lifted her head as the voice drifted to her across the table.

A couple of the girls Sam worked with at the mall bookstore had been walking past. Kelly recognized one of them as Marie, though she couldn't remember the other one's name.

"Hi!" she said.

The girls came closer. "How is Sam doing?" Marie asked quietly.

Kelly frowned, cocking her head a little. "What do you mean? When was the last time you saw her?"

Marie looked like she may have opened a door she hadn't wanted to. "Oh, um, well - Sam hasn't been to work for a couple of weeks. I'm not sure what happened," she said. She started to back away from the table. "Just tell her I said hey, okay?"

CHAPTER TWENTY-ONE

K elly was torn - she didn't want to drag more people into her sister's life, but she needed to know what was going on. She jumped up from the table. "Wait!" she whispered, reaching out one hand and grabbing Marie's sleeve. Marie looked back at her, fear flashing across her face. Kelly let go of her arm. "I'm sorry, please, wait," she said. "Something is going on, and I'm trying to figure out what. Sam was attacked this weekend - she's in the hospital."

Marie's hand flew to cover her mouth. "Oh, I'm so sorry," she whispered.

Her friend grabbed her other sleeve and gave a little tug. "Not here!" she breathed. Her eyes darted around the library.

Marie glanced at her friend, then back at Kelly. "Meet us in the back study cubbies in 15 minutes," she said so softly that Kelly almost missed it.

Nodding, Kelly sat back down. She returned her attention to her notebook as the girls continued their stroll toward the bathroom. What was that about? She racked her brain, trying to remember the other girl's name. Donna? Delia? Something that started with a D. Kelly had met Maria a couple of times over the past two years that Sam had worked at the store. It was a popular place for students to work part-time since there were so many students with such varying hours available to work. Marie had always seemed like a nice person. She was an English major, Kelly thought, remembering her focus on British authors the last time she had seen her at the store.

Kelly knew that Sam had not mentioned losing her job. That was what it sounded like Marie was saying - she said she wasn't sure what happened. Kelly snuck a glance at her phone to check the time. She still had eight minutes. She knew the study cubbies Marie was talking about - they had outlets to plug laptops into and cups of coffee were allowed. Standing up, Kelly strolled over to the new admission table and picked up a book. She turned it over to stare at the back, appearing to read the summary while she surreptitiously glanced around the room. Why had the other girl been so nervous to talk in the main lobby? There were a couple of students gathered at one table in the corner, pointing to diagrams of the circulatory system and muttering comments to each other. A young man sat on one of the couches with one ankle crossed on his knee, eyes closed and hands laced behind his head, listening to something through a set of headphones. A few more clusters of couples studying on stools at high top tables in front of the windows failed to raise her suspicions. She put the book down and picked up another. Turning her body a little, she noticed a man at the coffee vending machine with his back to her. He wore jeans and ratty sneakers, and a faded blue hoodie sweatshirt, unzipped. His brown hair was just curling up a little at the collar. Catching a glimpse of the side of his face as he bent to pick up his coffee, Kelly felt her chest constrict. She quickly turned her back to him and carried the book she held with her as she crossed the room to head into the stacks. She couldn't be 100 percent sure, but she was almost certain the man was the same man from the hospital the day before.

She walked partway down the aisle before ducking into one of the stacks. She stepped quickly to get to the other end and ducked behind the end of the stack, then stood silently for a minute or two, listening. She didn't hear any footsteps following her. She held her breath and risked turning the corner to see if he was trying to find her.

Waiting a few more moments, Kelly hurried to the study cubbies in the back room to find Marie and her friend. Marie was there, standing at the back of the sitting area.

"Diana had to go," she said, her eyes not meeting Kelly's. "Listen, I don't want to really get involved. I'm only here because Sam used to be a good kid, but I don't know much."

Kelly took a deep breath to quiet her frustration. "Please tell me whatever you know. I know that Sam had written some disturbing things were going on, and then she came home and was attacked, and as of this morning, she was still in a coma. Whatever you can tell me, it might help us figure out what is happening!" She spoke quietly but urgently.

Marie hesitated, then nodded. "A couple of months ago, Sam was taking a class - an online summer class that had something to do with local history. She started researching one of the legends, and then she started talking about really freaky stuff. A lot of people around here see things and hear things, and the townies all say it has to do with the legends and its best left alone. Sam said she didn't believe in the legends, and she didn't want to leave it alone." Marie looked around and lowered her voice even more, so that Kelly had to step closer to hear. "Then Sam started talking crazy. That's part of the legend. Nobody wanted her to mess with it, but she wouldn't stop, and she kept getting crazier. The store manager had to fire her - he said it was because she missed a shift, but he would have kept her on if it wasn't for the legends. And I know Sam, but honestly, she was acting like she was high or something some of the time."

Marie glanced at her watch. "I have to go, I have a class," she said. She tightened her hold on her book bag.

"Wait - do you know anything about Jill, Sam's roommate?" Kelly asked quickly.

Marie startled, looked around again, and shook her head. "I can't. I'm sorry. I hope Sam is okay, but I can't get into more of this." She stepped passed Kelly and walked quickly toward the side entrance of the library.

Kelly glanced around the study area and sank into a nearby chair. This had to all be tied into that stupid Skinwalker thing that Sam had been talking about. Frowning, she wondered if she could access any information on the legend online. A soft noise from behind her in

one of the stacks set her hair on end. Slowly, she stood and crept toward the stacks, trying to remain as quiet as possible. Rounding the
nearest corner, she spotted the back of a blue sweatshirt exiting the
other end.

CHAPTER TWENTY-TWO

Fear gripped her, tightening its grip on her heart. Who was the guy from the photos, and why was he messing around following her? Anger quickly replaced the fear. She didn't need more drama from this guy following her around and trying to listen in on her conversations! Kelly hurried to the end of the stack and looked down the aisle. She didn't see the blue sweatshirt. Moving quickly, she checked each row as she headed for the main lobby of the library. Climbing the steps to the entry, she saw the blue sweatshirt heading out the door. It was the same man that had been getting his coffee from the machine. Kelly sped across the library and caught the door as he hit the bottom of the stairs.

"Hey!" she shouted at him.

He ignored her, turning down the sidewalk and rounding the corner of the building. Kelly bounded after him, reaching out to grab the back of his sweatshirt a few steps down the side of the building.

"Hey!" she shouted again.

The man spun around, catching her wrist in his hand. His tousled hair and scruffy beard seemed at odds with the quick intelligence in his brown eyes. His grip prevented her from falling, caught short by his sudden stop, but also prevented her from stepping away from him.

"You don't want to do this," he said in a quiet undertone. "There's enough going on without you two getting hurt, too. Go home and leave things alone. Stay safe."

He abruptly let go of her wrist with a little shove, unbalancing her. He had taken two steps away before she managed to grab at his sweatshirt again. "Wait! What do you know?" she said, her voice not quiet but no longer shouting.

Sighing, he turned around again and took a step back toward her. Instinctively, Kelly felt a knot of fear tighten in her stomach.

111

The man was not a large man, but he moved in a way that spoke of control. His eyes swept the campus behind her quickly as he turned. "You need to let this go," he said. "You want your sister to be okay, you want your brother to be okay, then you need to get on that bus and go home and leave this alone. I can't give you anything more."

The fire in Kelly's stomach was spreading. He had to know what was going on - she had to make him tell her!

"Kelly!" a relieved shout from the front of the library caught her attention.

Kelly turned to see Wayne standing with the bicycle, one hand in the air to catch her attention. There were more students on the grounds now; classes must have just let out. She turned her attention back to the man, but he had taken advantage of her distraction and had disappeared into a crowd of students heading to the student center. Wayne rolled the bike up to her side.

"They had tubes there, and there was a guy who was chaining his bike up to the rack that helped me change the tube," he said, indicating the tire with grease streaked hands. "I need to go in and wash my hands. Who was that guy?"

"I don't know," Kelly moaned. "That is the guy who was at the hospital yesterday, and then today he was following me in the library! I followed him out here to find out why he is following us and he told me to leave things alone and go home, or else we'll end up in more trouble - we have to go after him!"

But as Kelly looked around again, she knew that it was useless. The few seconds it had taken to fill Wayne in had been enough for the man to disappear.

"Are you serious?" Wayne was astounded. "Kelly, are you crazy?"

Kelly turned back to look at Wayne, frustrated almost to the point of tears.

"Don't you see? This proves that Sam wasn't involved in whatever this is! Something big is going on," she said.

"Yeah, it proves that something dangerous is going on, Kel!" Wayne shot back. "We have enough to bring back to the police and let them handle it. Let's just bring the pictures and the rest of this back and let someone who's trained to deal with this do it. Do you want to end up like Sam?"

Kelly bit back a retort. "Sam lost her job because of this skin-walker legend - one of her friends from the bookstore told me in the library," she said. "She said no one will deal with any of the weird stuff that goes on because of the legend. How do we know that the police are going to be able to get anywhere?"

"Why do you think we can get anywhere if you don't think the police can get anywhere?" Wayne reached out to put his hand on Kelly's arm to make sure she was listening to him. "Kelly, you said we needed to come to Sam's to see what we could find so that the police would keep looking past the drugs in her system. We've got enough to get them to do that - we don't need to turn up hurt like Sam. Let's go back and turn this stuff in."

Wayne was insistent. Kelly hated that he was making sense - she wanted to chase that man down and make him tell her what was going on. Her anger that he had gotten away from her overshadowed the fear he had made her feel.

With Wayne tugging at her sleeve, Kelly agreed to head to the bike shop to return the bikes. The time in the library had taken longer than she thought - they would have to make good time to get to the shop before it closed. They went to the bike rack in front of the library where Kelly had left her bike. Looking down as she pulled the bike out of the rack, Kelly gasped.

"Someone's slit the tire!" she yelped.

Wayne quickly looked around. There was no one looking at them, though a couple of guys were hanging out at a picnic bench under a tree not too far away.

"Let's take it to the bookstore. I know where the bike stuff is - come on, just wheel it over," Wayne said in a quiet voice. He looked around again. "We need to get it fixed and get out of here, Kel."

Kelly pushed the bike wordlessly, following Wayne across the campus. Anger burned in her veins, making her hands shake a little as they walked.

Wayne returned quickly from inside the store with a tube for the tire and a screwdriver and a hand pump to blow the tire up.

"The cashier said I could borrow them - they keep them inside to work on decorations or something - I wasn't really listening. I told him I'd do it right here in front of the store and bring the tools right back," he said.

He unfastened the tire with the quick-mount attachment and soon had the tire off the rim. Someone had slit through the casing and the tube, but just replacing the tube would be enough to get them back to the bike shop. Kelly was probably going to lose some of the deposit she had put down, but she should get most of it returned. Wayne used the screwdriver to work the tire back over the rim and set to work pumping it up with the pump.

Kelly looked around the campus, searching for the man in the sweatshirt. One man leaned against the side of a building that announced it was the science pod, watching with idle curiosity as Wayne pumped the tire. He was wearing a tan jacket, though, and had dark blond hair. A couple sat on a bench in front of a sculpture of twisted metal. The girl had her dark head resting on his chest, his arm curled around her shoulders and resting at her waist. Dozens of other students walked in pairs and groups across the grounds, disappearing into buildings or heading to the parking lot. A couple of guys were pulling out packs of cigarettes as they neared the sidewalk approaching the front street.

Kelly turned and saw a couple of men heading toward a gray car in the parking lot. She started - it was the man with the blue sweatshirt! He was with another man in jeans and a sweater who opened the driver's side door, jangling car keys in his hand. He threw his head back and laughed, a barking sound that Kelly could hear across the lot. The man in the blue sweatshirt smiled and shook his head as he got into the passenger side of the car.

"Wayne! It's him!" Kelly said, pointing.

Wayne turned to look where she was pointing, then quickly grabbed her hand and pulled it down. "Kelly, quit pointing," he hissed.

"But it's the guy from the library, from the hospital!" Kelly argued. She wanted to run to the car, to scream - she didn't know.

"Kelly," Wayne's hiss was insistent. "See that other guy - the driver?"

"No, the one in the blue sweatshirt!" Kelly's voice was rising with her frustration.

"No, Kelly - listen!" Wayne grabbed her shoulder and shook her a little. "Do you see the driver? That is the guy that let me use his tools to change the tire on this bike," Wayne nudged the bike he had ridden with his foot. He looked at the other bikes standing in the bike rack. "Look - the bike he pulled up with is still here - it's the green one there. He seemed chatty, now that I think about it - I was so glad he was here with tools I could use it didn't register how talkative he was."

Wayne kept his hand on Kelly's shoulder as they watched the car pull out of the parking lot. It joined a string of others in the drive toward the campus exit. As the vehicle passed slowly in front of the grounds separating the bookstore from the street, the man with the sweatshirt looked at Kelly. He gave no sign of recognition, then spoke an answer to the driver of the car before turning away.

Wayne dropped his hand and finished pumping the bike tire up. "We are going home. Now. Okay?" he asked.

Kelly nodded without answering. She fished in her messenger bag and pulled out a pen and her notebook, writing "8GN" on the cover. She hadn't been able to see the whole license plate, but maybe this would be better than nothing. There was nothing more they could do from here, today, and it was becoming more evident that whatever this was, it was bigger than she had thought. If the driver of the car had pretended to have a bike so that he could use helping Wayne to fix the tire as a way to talk to him, he must be involved, too.

"Wayne - was that the car from Sam's apartment?" Kelly asked when Wayne came back outside after returning the screwdriver and hand pump to the store clerk.

"No - the car at Sam's was dark brown, either a Nissan or a Honda, I couldn't see which," he said.

"What was this one?" she asked, preparing to write his answer down next to the partial plate number she had written.

"Honda, a civic, I think," he said. Wayne was a car geek, though more when it came to American classics.

Kelly nodded, making the notation. If they were going to go back and hand everything over to the police, she wanted to make sure she had done as much as she could to catch the men who had hurt Sam. She quickly stowed the notebook back in her bag and swung her leg over the bike seat. They would really need to put some muscle behind their pedaling if they were going to make it back to the bike shop now before it closed.

Wayne pulled out his phone and tapped in the name of the bike shop. Kelly had thought they would need to go back by way of Sam's apartment to get back, but it turned out there was a side road that would shave nearly 15 minutes off their route. Kicking off, they maneuvered out of the school campus and followed the voiced directions from the GPS.

"Wayne, can you remember what the driver was talking about when he helped you change the tube of your bike?" Kelly asked as they rode.

Wayne looked thoughtful. "He asked if I lived near campus – said if we couldn't fix the bike he could get me a lift home. I told him I was visiting my sister. He asked who she was, wanted to know if maybe he knew her. I told him Sam's name – I thought if he did know her, he might be able to tell me something, you know? But he said he didn't recognize the name." Wayne pedaled a little without speaking as he crested a small hill. "He suggested that if I was going to be around for a few days that he could hook me up with a party, but I said I was only here for the day. He asked where I was from, but I figured if he didn't recognize Sam's name, I didn't really need him knowing more about me, so I told him I was from Riverside. I don't know, Kelly. I can't think of anything else, really."

Kelly mulled his words. Why would one of the men involved in hurting Sam act like he didn't know who she was? He was with the guy in the sweatshirt, so he had to be involved, right? She shook her head. She needed to write things down to be able to make more sense of them. When they were on the bus headed back home she would be able to focus a little better on it.

CHAPTER TWENTY-THREE

They took another turn at the GPS' prompting. The voice announced that they should arrive at the bike shop in nine minutes. Kelly smirked. It always seemed like a challenge to her when she used the GPS in her car, and it told her how long it should take her to reach her destination - she always made it where she was heading in less time than the GPS estimated. They were passing houses at regular intervals now, and blocks were more regular. They were nearing the center of town. She pushed her legs a little harder. Kelly knew where the bike shop was now, she recognized the grocery store she had gone to with Sam to pick up food the week she had visited. The bike shop would be two blocks down, on a side street near the gas station. They were going to make it just before closing time.

Wayne showed the shop attendant the tires he had repaired. The tire on the bike he had fallen with was still in good shape, with just a scratch on the fork and another on hate handlebar. The tire on Kelly's bike would have to be replaced, though. The attendant took off the price for a new tire and issued a return for the remainder of the deposit that Kelly had given him at the start of the day.

"I know it can't cost that much for a new tire, but I suppose I have to pay for the labor of having him take the tire apart to put the new tread on, too," Kelly grumbled as she and Wayne walked back toward the bus stop.

"It was still a better way to get around than walking, and cheaper than taking a cab," Wayne pointed out. He had his backpack in his arms, one hand rummaging inside. "Looks like I'm out of food. Want to grab something in that coffee shop before the bus comes?"

Kelly shrugged. She hadn't noticed herself getting hungry, but now that Wayne brought it up, she supposed that it wouldn't be long before she was. "Yeah, okay. We'll have to get it to go, though - the bus should be here in 20 minutes or so."

Wayne pulled open the coffee shop door and led the way inside. He pulled his phone partially out of his pocket, glanced at the screen, and pushed it back into his pocket.

"Who is it?" Kelly asked.

"Mom," he said. "She's been texting me to see if I need a ride home from practice. I figured I would text her when we get on the bus and tell her I'm all set." He walked up to the counter and glanced around.

The waitress from earlier in the day was not there. A dark-haired woman shouted that she would be right over. When they had ordered drinks and sandwiches, they walked to a small table to wait for their food to be made. Kelly glanced around at the other patrons; the crowd was lighter this late in the afternoon. A couple of college students with laptops sat at the stools occupied by the students earlier in the day; Kelly figured those must be the seats closest to the electrical outlets.

A couple of middle-aged women, elegantly coiffed and elaborately painted, sat sipping coffee at another small table. Kelly gazed, transfixed. She was used to elaborate make-up. In the theater, if an actor wasn't wearing a lot of make-up, he would look washed out and weak. She had worked backstage for school plays in high school and college. She wasn't accustomed to such heavy make-up being worn in public places, though. Tearing her gaze from the women, she stared at a bookshelf on the back wall as though she were trying to read the titles of the books and tried to overhear the women's conversation. From the few disjointed words she could make out, the two were heading to a showing of a play hosting its opening night a few towns over.

"Are you sure he won't be offended?" The women were making their way to the exit. "You know him better than I, but I've not heard of anyone dressing as a character from a play to go see it," one woman said.

"I think he'll be positively astounded," assured the other. "He'll see this as the flattery it is meant as, I promise. What playwright wouldn't want to know how much his audience is touched by his characters?"

The women exited the shop. Kelly looked at Wayne, expecting to see her own amusement mirrored on his face, but he was checking his phone and hadn't noticed.

"What's up?"

"Not much," he said. He pushed the phone back into his pocket as the waitress brought their food, packaged to go. "Thank you, very much," he smiled at the woman, who smiled warmly, nodded, and headed back to the counter as Kelly stood to go.

Kelly took her coffee. She grabbed the bag with her sandwich and put it at the top of her messenger bag, then stepped out the door. There was a bench in front of the shop they could sit on while waiting for the bus. She blew through the hole in the top of the cup and took a sip of her coffee as she made herself comfortable on the bench, then grimaced.

"Oh, this is black! I've got to get sugar and cream, I'll be right back," she said, jumping back up and leaving Wayne grinning at her, lifting his foamy, perfectly mixed drink in mock toast.

Kelly went back inside and found a table to the side of the counter equipped with sugar and cream. She fixed her coffee, grimacing as she took a couple of sips to make enough room in the cup to add the cream. She still overfilled the cup and hastily grabbed some napkins to wipe up the puddle. She sipped again before putting the cover back on to make sure it was up to par, then wiped down the side of the cup and ran another napkin over the table top to make sure she had gotten all of the mess she had made. She glanced at the clock on the wall near the counter before turning to rejoin Wayne outside, then froze. Through the window, she could see a gray car parked in the spot in front of the bus stop sign. She moved toward the door quickly, splashing hot coffee on her hand as she pushed the door open.

A man with an unkempt beard sat in the driver's seat of the car. It was the same man who had driven past them on their way to the school. A brown haired man stood on the sidewalk with his hands in his pants pockets, talking to Wayne. As Kelly stepped out of the coffee shop, he turned to look at her. Nodding once at her, he turned back to Wayne. "I wouldn't want it to go badly, you understand?" He glanced again at Kelly, looked deliberately at Wayne, and walked purposefully to the passenger side of the car. As he stooped to get in the vehicle, the bus drove up the street and pulled in behind the car.

Wayne stood, grabbed his backpack, and walked to the door of the bus wordlessly. Kelly caught up to him as he boarded the bus and handed over his ticket. They made their way to the rear of the bus, which was much less crowded than the bus that morning had been.

CHAPTER TWENTY-FOUR

"What was that?" Kelly asked tensely as she sat next to him. Wayne glanced around. He reached over and put his hand on hers, squeezing tightly briefly before releasing her. He shook his head as though a shudder of cold ran through him. "How is your coffee, were you able to fix it?"

Kelly started. She looked at Wayne quizzically. He was staring out the window at the gray car, which had not pulled into traffic yet. He turned back to look at her and widened his eyes for a split second before looking normal at her coffee. "I finished mine outside, but I'm going to eat my sandwich now. I still have half a bottle of water left, so I'm good."

Kelly was clearly missing something. She decided to go along with his antics for the moment. She leaned her head back against the headrest on the back of her seat and looked slowly around the bus. Including the bus driver, there were only half a dozen other people on the bus, each sitting alone. Two had headphones in their ears, one with eyes closed and hand tapping his thigh along with the beat, the other staring unblinkingly out the window. Another man had his eyes closed, his head leaning against the window of the bus as he dozed. One woman was engrossed in a book, her lips mouthing the words as she read, one finger sliding down the page to help her keep track.

A thin woman was chewing the skin near her thumbnail and staring out the window at the coffee shop. She wore jeans and a flannel shirt over a light t-shirt. Kelly frowned, then worked to mask her expression. It had been warm enough out during the day, but now that the sun was going down, it was starting to get chilly. This girls' flip-flops would definitely not be Kelly's choice of footwear this late in the fall.

Wayne was digging his sandwich out of his backpack. He set the bag down on the floor near his feet, then reconsidered and stuck it between his arm and the side of the bus. He glanced around as he did so but said nothing. He unwrapped his sandwich from the paper it was wrapped in, using the paper as a plate of sorts in his lap. He took a bite and chewed, though he appeared to have a hard time swallowing.

Kelly slowly unwrapped her own sandwich, following Wayne's example and using the wrapping as a plate in her lap. She looked at the turkey sandwich with dismay. It was stuffed with meat, had a decent slathering of mayo under the lettuce and tomato, and would have otherwise been very tempting after all the exercise she had gotten that day, but her appetite had fled with the brown-haired man's arrival. She picked up one half of the sandwich and raised it to her mouth, but lowered it again. She didn't feel like she could eat, and it wouldn't do any of them any good for her to choke on the bus ride home. She rewrapped the sandwich and tucked it back into her bag. "I think I'll wait a bit," she said. She lifted the cup to her lips and managed a sip of coffee, not looking at Wayne.

The bus driver had gotten off the bus at the stop and gone into the coffee shop. He hurried out to the bus and climbed back into his seat, stowing a cup of coffee in a cup holder at the dashboard. He glanced into the mirror and made eye contact with Kelly briefly before glancing away. He used his mirrors to pull out into traffic, neatly avoiding the gray car that was still parked in front of the sign. The stop had taken just a couple of extra minutes, but Kelly thought her nerves had been stretched an extra mile. She turned to Wayne, expecting him to talk now that they were away from the stop, but he gave a quick shake of his head and took another bite of sandwich. His eyes strayed to the thin girl at the front, still picking at her thumb, and then to the bus driver. He put the sandwich down in his lap and reached into his backpack, withdrawing the half-finished bottle of water.

"Just wait. Not here," he whispered as he brought the bottle to his lips to take a sip.

Kelly sighed and turned her head toward the other side of the bus. Whatever the brown-haired man had said to Wayne, and obviously it had to be something about what was going on, Kelly needed to get some of this sorted before they got home. Her parents were going to find out where they had gone, and they had better be able to give them some answers that made sense. She pulled out her phone. She could at least try to figure out what the skinwalker legends were about while she waited for Wayne to calm down.

Half an hour later, Kelly was growing increasingly frustrated. Trying to search for information on the Internet on her phone was not as easy as on her laptop, but she had never failed this spectacularly before. She tried putting in different keywords but was only seeing returns of native American legends out West having to do with Native Americans with abilities to assume forms of animals - nothing local to the area, really, and nothing tying the legends to drugs.

Kelly thought about the journal entries Jill had written, and searched for pink pills and depression, warm, cozy, and other words that Jill had used to describe the effects of the drugs. With this, she thought she was having a little more luck. Several images showed up with the caption "MDMA," and there were even links to pages offering to sell the pills based on her location. Kelly frowned, her eyebrows pulling down. She swiped down on the screen and disabled the locator app on the phone. She would prefer to be able to do her sleuthing anonymously - or at least not advertise her whereabouts as she was doing it.

The bus slowed and lurched sidewards toward a bus stop sign, stopping abruptly. Kelly put a hand out to steady herself on the seat in front of her and looked up at the front of the bus. The thin girl with the bitten thumbnails was moving down the stairs. Kelly saw the bus driver's mouth move as he said something to her. The girl made no indication that she heard him as she swung out the door and walked down the sidewalk. This bus stop was in front of a park. Kelly watched through the window as the girl cut through some low-growing bushes to step into the park. She avoided the paved walkways to walk toward a stand of trees, disappearing from Kelly's view as the bus resumed its route.

Kelly glanced around. The girl reading the book was gone, as was the man who had tapped to the beat of whatever song he was listening to. A few other passengers had boarded the bus, all absorbed in their own travels. She must have missed a couple of stops while she was focused on researching the legend.

"Kelly," Wayne spoke her name quietly. He had his elbow leaning on the window and his hand resting on his face, covering his mouth discreetly. "Don't look at me, just listen, okay?"

Kelly picked up her phone and switched to Facebook, then held it in front of her like a book and pretended interest in the screen.

Wayne continued in a voice so low she had to shift a little closer to hear him. She put her elbow on the armrest between them and crossed her foot under her other leg, aiming for the picture of leisure as she scrolled her news feed.

• • • •

"WHEN YOU WENT IN TO fix your coffee, those guys pulled up in the car," Wayne said. "The guy that got out was Mark - he said he was Jill's better half. He said the other guy had seen some bikes at the apartment, and then seen us on the bikes on the way to the school and got concerned that something might be wrong with Sam. The way he started out, if we didn't know better, I might have thought he was concerned about her. That changed quickly, though - he could see you through the window of the coffee shop. He said it gets really hard on a guy when his sister gets hurt. Kel, the guy is a sociopath. He's just talking like he's asking how the weather is, but he's saying how it would probably be difficult to live with yourself if your stupidity got your sister gutted like a deer in hunting season - that's what he said! Then you must have started looking like you were coming out soon because he said he has people everywhere. He has people who don't look like they would know anything or anyone, and he's keeping an eye on us. Then he said that bit about not wanting it to go badly when you came outside."

Wayne went quiet. Kelly risked a glance at him - his eyes were closed, and he looked as though he had fallen asleep. She knew he hadn't - his breathing was still shallow, and the hand in his lap clenched. Kelly felt the rising panic in her own throat and fought to contain it. She glanced at the front of the bus and caught the bus driver's gaze in the mirror again. The man who had been staring out the window with the earbuds in was looking back at them. He didn't look away when he saw her looking at him, staring insolently back for a moment before one side of his mouth lifted in a smirk.

Kelly looked away. Maybe Mark was making idle threats - what kind of person says he has people everywhere? On the other hand, though, he had followed Sam home, and found Kelly and Wayne. That was pretty coincidental if he didn't have people everywhere, watching. But, what if it was just the guy in the sweatshirt? He had been in the photo with Sam. He had been at the hospital, Kelly was sure of it. And today he had been in the library at the college. He could be the only person watching them, and Mark could have found out through him.

Kelly looked back down at her phone.

She still had her Facebook news feed open. Someone had posted a quote, but it was the photo in the background that first caught her eye - it was a picture of a woman caught in a rainstorm, her hair and clothes plastered to her body from the downpour. Superimposed over the image were the words, "The Lord will carry you through the storm." Kelly paused. Slowly, she touched the screen. The image jumped to fill the screen, and Kelly reread the verse. She tapped the link to bring her to the page that had posted the quote and watched the screen. If there ever was a storm in her life, this was it - and she could use some reassurance that she remained in the hands of a God who was bigger than this storm.

"Sometimes life is overwhelming - health problems arise, or relationships hit rocky patches, or maybe job responsibilities threaten to crush us," the blogger had written. "When you find yourself in that space, find comfort in this verse - Isaiah 43:2, 'When you pass through the waters I will be with you When you cross rivers you will not drown. When you walk through the fire you will not be burned, nor will the flames hurt you. This is because I, the Lord, am your God, the Holy One of Israel, your Savior.' How amazing that you can be in the middle of a furious storm, and yet trust that the creator of the world is bigger than the creation. God is in control, and when we remember that, we are able to find rest - even though the storm rages around us."

Kelly closed her eyes. She loved the number of times that she would be having a stressful day and, seemingly out of nowhere, along would come a reminder that she wasn't alone. She took a few deep breaths and sent up a silent prayer of thanks that God cared enough to tap her on the shoulder and slow her down. Opening her eyes, she saw that the man with the earbuds was looking at her again. She gave him a brilliant smile before turning and nudging Wayne. She handed Wayne her phone, still open to the devotional. She watched him read it and pause, then reread it. He gave her back her phone with a weak smile. Kelly smiled back - it was small, but any little encouragement would help.

Ear Buds, as Kelly had taken to calling him, got off the bus before it got to the central station. She and Wayne disembarked, conscious of the eyes of the bus driver on their retreating backs. They scanned the boards listing the buses and their corresponding routes quickly, finding theirs and making their way over to it before speaking.

"Wayne, you don't have to worry. He's not going to hurt Sam or me again. We're going to figure this out," Kelly said.

Wayne grunted. He looked like he had more to say, but closed his mouth as he glanced around them. "Did you see all those people on the bus? How many of them were looking at us? He could have people watching us now," he said.

Kelly shook her head. "How? Everyone that was on the bus when we got on, got off before this station. Who could he have watching us?"

Wayne had been thinking about that. "The bus driver got off the bus, and then looks our way when he gets back on - and that was at the bus stop where Mark was. The skinny chick - she was obviously an addict, probably promised a fix for reporting back. The creepy guy who kept looking at you - any one of them or even all of them could have been watching us for him. And here," Wayne looked around wildly, "he could have texted anyone and told them to watch for us to show up! No, Kel, I'm serious!" Wayne shook his head as Kelly started to laugh.

"What if he did? What are they going to tell him, that we got off a bus and got on a bus? Seriously, Wayne, you're making this bigger than it is," she said.

"Am I?" Wayne's face was set. "Sam's in the hospital because this isn't as big as I think? No, Kelly, I don't think I'm wrong. You didn't hear that guy - he's off, and he's dangerous. And we're going to be careful."

The bus driver opened the door and began allowing passengers to board. They climbed the stairs and handed in their tickets, then made their way to seats at the back of the bus. There were a few more passengers on this bus than the last, but they were still on their way within minutes.

CHAPTER TWENTY-FIVE

Kelly looked at Wayne and knew she would not be able to change his mind about how much danger they might be in. Switching subjects, she asked, "Did you text Mom?"

Color drained from Wayne's face. "Oh, no! Oh, man, I forgot! Crap!"

"Well, they're going to know we weren't at school when we get home, anyway," Kelly said. "But we probably ought to call now, because they probably are already worried sick."

She pulled out her phone and swiped the screen to wake it up, noticing that she had several text messages she hadn't noticed coming in. She scanned the texts and sighed, then called up the phone contacts and dialed her mother's cell.

"Mom already knows something is up - she texted me a bunch of times," she told Wayne as she waited for the call to connect. Her mother picked up the phone on the second ring. "Hi, Mom. I know - yes, he's with me. We're okay. I'm sorry. I know, but Mom - okay. No, I know. Yes. Um," she pulled the phone away to glance at the phone, then put it back to her ear. "We should be at the bus stop in about 25 minutes. Okay, thank you. Mom, wait - how is Sam?" Kelly had closed her eyes to focus on her mother's voice, trying not to sound defensive. "Okay. See you in a bit."

She hit the button to hang up the phone and looked up at Wayne's face. "Well, so they know already that we didn't go to school," she said weakly. "And they are not happy. She said she had to call the police to let them know that we are safe, since they had already called to file missing person reports. Sam woke up, though. For a couple of hours this afternoon, so that's good news."

Kelly slumped back in her seat. Wayne sat quietly, picking at the seam of his jeans with his fingernail. The ride seemed much faster than it had that morning.

As they dismounted the bus, Kelly glanced around. She spotted her father's truck in front of the station and headed for it. Wayne followed closely, surveying the area as he walked. Kelly wondered if he was expecting more of those creatures to show up, like a repeat of Sam's adventure. If he did, he would be disappointed, as there were no unexpected lurkers around.

Kelly opened the passenger side door of the truck and steeled herself for the onslaught. Instead, her father's chilly silence filled the cab. She climbed into the back seat, allowing Wayne the front seat for his long legs. Her father started the truck and pulled out into traffic without a word. Wayne looked back at Kelly and then at Dad.

"Dad," Kelly began, but he cut her off.

"Wait. I don't want to hear a thing until we're with your mother. Just - don't."

Kelly subsided. Her insides squirmed, feeling like a vice was gripping her somewhere in her middle and squeezing. She knew her parents would be upset if they found out what she had planned, but somehow that knowledge hadn't translated into this heart-wrenching pain of their disapproval. Her father's upright posture, his tight grip on the steering wheel, his stony silence were proof that she had wounded him. Wayne looked somehow curled into himself on the front seat, though he sat silently staring out the window. Kelly knew that she was responsible for his pain, too, that he would never have gone to Sam's without her. He would likely never have thought of it. She looked down, staring at her hands in her lap.

The truck pulled to a stop. Dad put it in park and pulled the keys out, opening his door in one fluid motion. Kelly looked up, confused to be at the hospital, and then surprised at her confusion. Of course they were at the hospital - Mom would still be with Sam. Wayne opened his door and jumped out, pulling the seat forward to allow Kelly to climb out. They looked into each other's eyes for a moment before silently following Dad up the sidewalk to the hospital.

Dad walked directly to the elevator and punched the button. The hospital was quiet; most visitors came by during the afternoon and went home before now. They rode up in the elevator, the small, confined space making the silence even bigger between them. The doors slid open, and Dad walked quickly and directly to Sam's room. Kelly and Wayne followed. Dad opened the door quietly, moving the curtain aside and walking over to sit on the edge of the chair Mom was in. He reached down to take her hand as Kelly and Wayne entered the room. They looked around - to Kelly, the place seemed the same as yesterday when they had left, other than the frigid reception from their parents' stiff demeanor.

Mom looked at Kelly and Wayne for a moment before speaking. When she did speak, her voice shook with anger.

"I want to hear what you could possibly have had to do today that you felt was so important to sneak off without telling us. I do," she said, struggling to keep her voice even. "And I will try to keep an open mind and hear what you have to say. But I want you to know that we have been through more in the past three days than we have been through in a lifetime, and the thought that we have raised children who would know what we have been through and deliberately choose to inflict more worry and stress on us is a very bitter pill to swallow. So, please, I want no lies. I want no persuasions. I want just facts, and I want just truth."

Kelly glanced at Wayne. He was staring at his shoes, his face pale. As many times as the school had called about the trouble he had been caught in, as many times as the two of them had gotten scolded over things growing up, they had never seen their mother this angry. As scary as Dad was when he yelled and waved his hands, he was a teddy bear compared to this Mom.

Looking back at her parents, Kelly began.

"I wanted to help Sam," she said.

Wayne lifted his head and looked at her.

"We both did," Kelly amended. "We thought that when the hospital found the drugs in her system, the police would think that she was just a junkie or something, and they wouldn't look any further. But Sam's not a junkie - we know she's not!" Kelly fought to keep the emotion out of her voice, to match her mother's even delivery. She took a deep breath to steady herself. "We went to Sam's apartment to see if we could find anything."

She waited, looking at her mother. She wanted to show them the pictures she had taken and tell them about the people they had seen, but she wasn't sure if finding proof that someone was behind what had happened to Sam would work for them or against them at this point.

"You thought going to Sam's apartment without telling anyone where you were going was smart?" Dad asked, his voice rising. "We talked to your friends - none of them knew anything! What if something had happened to you? We wouldn't have had any idea to even start looking out there!"

Kelly hung her head. "I'm sorry," she said. He did have a point - an even bigger point than he knew.

"I have been sitting here all afternoon, wondering if you were laying on the ground somewhere, if those animals or people or whatever they were had gotten you, too," Mom said. Her voice broke on the last words and tears spilled out over her lashes. "We called your friends. We called the police. We have been frantic - and you've been, what, sitting on the bus, too busy to call and let us know you were safe!"

"Mom, no," Wayne said. "We didn't want you worried! We thought we could just go there and get some proof and come back - we're sorry!" He moved quickly and was kneeling at Mom's side before she had uncovered her face. Wayne put a hand on Mom's shoulder and she reached for him, capturing him in a crushing hug.

Kelly, feeling left out, sidled forward and sat on the edge of Sam's bed.

"I'm really sorry," she said, looking back and forth between Mom and Dad. Meeting Dad's eyes, she continued, "I didn't think the whole thing through. I was just so focused on getting something to help Sam, I wasn't thinking about how worried you would be if you found out we had gone."

Dad shook his head. Kelly could see his disgust, but also his relief that they had returned unhurt.

Mom raised her head and released her grip on Wayne. Wiping her face of tears, she sat back and surveyed the two of them. "I have to say this before we move on and it doesn't get said. We have to be able to trust each other - you both know that. I am shaken, today, more than I thought possible, in that trust. I don't know what to do with this, and you have to know that."

Kelly met Mom's eyes. She felt like the ground had shifted underneath her. Tears slipped down her cheeks.

Mom's mouth quivered, then tightened. She took a deep breath and met Wayne's eyes. She closed her eyes as more tears fell.

Dad put his hand on Mom's shoulders and squeezed reassurance to her. Clearing his throat, he asked, "What did you find?"

Kelly wiped her cheeks with her hands and looked at him. She felt raw and exposed. She glanced at Wayne, wondering if their answers were going to make this scene even worse. Although, she thought, as she reached into her bag for her phone, she wasn't sure anything could make this worse. She pushed the button on the side of her phone to turn the screen on, but it stayed black. Frowning, she hit it again, but the phone was off.

She closed her eyes. "The battery is dead."

"We found drugs," said Wayne, his voice hoarse. He cleared his throat. "In Jill's room, we found pot, and pills, and a couple of boxes of what looked like mummified hands - body parts. And, we ran into

Jill's boyfriend, Mark, who threatened us." He looked at Kelly defiantly with the last statement, a silent challenge.

CHAPTER TWENTY-SIX

After much discussion, Kelly and Wayne agreed to take the photos and information they had gathered to the police in the morning. Dad insisted that he would drive them, and then take Wayne to school when they were done. Secretly, Kelly wondered if that was to make sure that Wayne actually went to school, but even though the atmosphere in the room had lifted, she didn't voice the jest.

Mom stretched, one hand at the small of her back, and rolled her head from side to side. She had slept for two nights in the chair in Sam's room, and her body was clearly aching.

"Mom, let me stay with Sam tonight," Kelly suggested. At her mother's lifted eyebrow, Kelly pressed on. "You need a night's sleep in a real bed. I promise I'll stay with her until you come back tomorrow. Let me do this, please."

Mom hesitated, but Dad spoke up. "Deb, let her stay. Sam woke up, she's doing better. You need to sleep." He smiled at her and said, "Frankly, you could do with a shower, too."

Mom laughed and reluctantly nodded. "Fine, stay with her. Kelly," she said, waiting until Kelly met her eyes before continuing, "I love you."

Kelly smiled, her heart lifting.

Wayne and their parents left, with Mom promising to be back with breakfast and Dad noting that they would hit the police station directly after.

Kelly sank into the chair Mom had been using at the side of Sam's bed, then jumped up again. She fished her phone charger out of her bag and found an outlet, then plugged the phone in and left it sitting on the bedside table which she pulled over. Electrical outlets appeared to be at a premium in hospital rooms, she mused, noting a couple behind the head of the bed with notices on them that they were for emergency use. She followed the cords that were plugged into those outlets with her eyes and found them attached to the bed and the i.v. stand. She surmised that those outlets must be connected to a generator source, in case of an outage.

She nestled back into the chair, leaned her head back, and closed her eyes. She was too wound up to sleep, but she hadn't been able to sort things on the bus. She could do that now.

"Kelly? Kelly, where's Mom and Dad? Kel?"

The soft questions were slow and punctuated with pauses, as though Sam was having trouble forming the words. Kelly opened her eyes without comprehension. Her neck was sore, having stretched to one side with the weight of her drooping head. She rolled her head back and around to the other side to ease the soreness from her sleeping position. As she did, she recognized the hospital room.

"Sam!" Kelly sat up abruptly, her confusion evaporated.

Sam lay drowsing on the pillow, blinking as she tried to clear her head of the fog of sleep. "Hey, Kelly," she murmured.

Kelly leaned forward and grasped Sam's hand on the bed. "Sam, thank God, you're awake! Mom and Dad went home so Mom could get some sleep - she's been here with you since you came in by ambulance. What time is it?" Kelly looked around for a clock. She reached for her cell phone on the tray table, but it was still powered off from when she had drained the battery earlier. Swiveling her head around to look at the walls, she found the clock next to the door. "Nearly midnight. Sam, how are you feeling?"

Sam was still slowly blinking her eyes—first one eye, then the other. She frowned in concentration. "Kel, I think something's wrong with my eyes. Everything is really blurry. I think it might be blurrier in my left eye, but it's hard to tell." Her voice was thick with sleep.

"Want me to ring for the nurse?"

"No. No, don't," she moved her hand fretfully as Kelly reached for the call light cord. When Kelly pulled her hand back, she said, "Kel, I want to tell you something. It's important. Do you believe me?"

Kelly squeezed her hand. "Of course I believe you, Sam. What is it?"

Sam lifted her head from the pillow and moved her eyes laboriously around the room, ensuring they were alone. "Kel, I'm not crazy."

Kelly stared at Sam's face, waiting.

"Sam, I don't think you're crazy, I believe you. What do you want to tell me?"

Sam focused her eyes on Kelly's. "I told you. I'm not crazy. Someone is trying to make me seem that way, but I know, I'm not crazy."

Kelly nodded, sitting back a little but not releasing Sam's hand. "I know, Sam. I know you're not crazy. I went to your apartment today."

Sam's eyes flew open. She struggled to lift her head, to move into a sitting position, then groaned against the pain in her arm. "You...what? Kelly... could have seen...could have gotten you - oh, God, this hurts!"

"Sam, it's okay. We're fine," Kelly said, trying to calm her. "Stop, let me put the head of the bed up, it'll be easier for you and won't hurt so much."

Sam stopped struggling and closed her eyes as Kelly pressed the button to raise the head of the bed. She moved her good hand up to her face, rubbing her forehead and temple as though to ease a headache before covering her mouth. Taking a deep, slow breath, she opened her eyes again and tried to focus on Kelly's face.

"Kelly, something strange is going on," she said, dropping her hand. Her voice was stronger but still as though she was having trouble moving her mouth's muscles. "Everyone told me...leave it alone, but...couldn't. Starting feeling strange. Losing hours...food was bitter...stopped eating at home. Got fired. People thought...drugs. I never...you know," she had closed her eyes while she was talking, but opened them again. "Then, started seeing...things. In the shadows, at first. And then Jill."

Tears welled in Sam's eyes and spilled over. She made no attempt to wipe them.

"Pictures, on my phone," she said, "but...so afraid to go back. I printed them at the library, bought...ticket home. I didn't think. They followed me," she closed her eyes again. "I'm so sorry," she whispered.

"Sam, we know you're not crazy, and this is not your fault," Kelly said, squeezing her hand. "We've seen the pictures. We gave them to the police after someone TP'd the house. Today, Wayne and I went to your apartment, and then to your school. You were right, something is going on - and we have proof! We took pictures!"

Kelly used her free hand to grab her cell phone again, this time hitting the button to turn it on. She hadn't had time to look through the photos since her phone had shut down on the bus ride home, and she'd apparently fallen asleep after plugging it in to charge.

They watched the screen as it played the startup sequence, then Kelly tapped the icon to open her photos. Seeing the little thumbnails renewed Kelly's apprehension.

"Sam, do you know what is in Jill's room?" She watched as Sam's eyes flicked to Kelly's face and then back to the phone's screen. "The drugs, and the rest?"

"I know Jill smokes, but...not...at the apartment," Sam said, then inhaled a slow gasp as Kelly enlarged one of the photos of the boxes of body parts in Jill's closet. "Oh my God. No."

Kelly nodded, scrolling through the pictures so that Sam could see them.

"Sam," Kelly hesitated, not wanting to hurt her sister but knowing it would come out soon anyway. "They tested your blood, and it came up positive for drugs, but they couldn't tell what with the test they ran.

Sam's face flushed. "I didn't take drugs," she said slowly, "but I did think...in my food. That's why..."

"That's why you stopped eating at home, and why you wrote in your journal that the milk tasted funny and you poured it out even though it was new," said Kelly, quickly filling in where her sister's plodding train of thought was headed. "You could be right - it would explain a lot of your symptoms, but I don't think weed would make you lose time, or see things, would it?"

Kelly shook her head. "Anyway, the blood tests are why Wayne and I went to your apartment. We knew you wouldn't do drugs, but we were afraid the police wouldn't look any further if they thought you did. We are going to give all of this to the police in the morning." Kelly motioned to the picture still visible on her screen.

Sam nodded slowly, rubbing at her temple again.

"Sam, let me ring for the nurse. You have a headache," Kelly said.

When Sam nodded again, Kelly used the call light to signal for the nurse and lowered the head of the bed.

After the nurse had been in with some pain meds and a glass of water, Kelly turned out the overhead light. "Sam, get some sleep. I'm not going anywhere tonight. In the morning, you'll feel better, and maybe be able to think more clearly. We'll get through this." She reached over and squeezed Sam's hand, adding, "God will protect us. He always does."

CHAPTER TWENTY-SEVEN

K elly strode quickly across the foyer of the police station, then stood back as a police officer escorted an older woman through the front door.

"We have the forms available right over here, ma'am," he was saying, directing her with his free hand while his other hand gently guided her under the elbow. "The assailant has a head start on us, but filing this report will at least get your insurance started on your claim."

Kelly didn't hear the rest of the officer's remarks. She pushed open the door again and stepped outside. Just what she needed, another reason for her father to be angry with her. She took a breath as she glanced around for the truck, then stepped down off the stairs and followed the sidewalk around to the parking lot. Dad and Wayne were already in the truck waiting for her.

"Where is your bag? You said you left it inside and had to go get it," Dad asked.

Kelly shook her head. "It wasn't in the room we waited in, or in the room where we talked to the detective. Let me look in the truck again."

Dad sighed and shook his head. "Kelly, I don't see how you can lose things so quickly. You had it when we left the hospital?"

Wayne hopped down from the front seat and pulled the seat forward so that Kelly could climb in the back. As he did, a corner of her small brown purse was exposed under the seat. "Is this it? I'm sorry, Kel," he said, pulling it free and handing it to her.

Kelly scowled at him pointedly. She climbed into the back seat. "It's fine, Dad. Can we just go?

Kelly leaned her head back on the headrest and closed her eyes as Dad pulled the truck into traffic and headed for the high school. The morning had not started out well. Kelly had not slept comfortably in the hospital, with nurses and aides coming in and out of the room every hour or so, and the chair that formed a bed of sorts was nothing like her bed at home. She was glad, though, that she had stayed and sent her mother home. When Sam's breakfast tray had come in, one of the nurse's aides had brought Kelly a coffee and muffin from the coffee shop in the hospital vestibule. Kelly knew the hospital staff was going above and beyond for her family and vowed to bring in a fruit basket or something for them before Sam was finally discharged. When Mom, Dad, and Wayne had arrived, Dad had been impatient to bring their evidence to the police station. Wayne had been rolling his eyes at Kelly behind Dad's back, so Kelly knew he'd already gotten an earful that morning before they left home. The final straw had been the detective's anger when they showed him the pictures of what they had seen in Sam's apartment, and Dad had pushed Wayne into telling about the encounters on campus and the bus stop.

"Do you kids realize how much danger you put yourselves in? How much damage you might have done to our case? If these guys know you were in that apartment, chances are they've already cleaned everything out of it. Even with your pictures, it is still basically your word against theirs - and you've put your fingerprints all over everything there, too," he said. "Look, I appreciate the fact you love your sister, but now you need to let us do our jobs. Don't make it harder on us by getting into the middle of things."

They had been quiet on the way out to the truck, but Kelly had panicked when she realized she didn't have her purse with her. She had been looking at the pictures on her phone on the ride over from the hospital; the bag must have slipped under the seat without her noticing it. She had promised to be quick and rushed back into the police station, pausing at the desk to be buzzed into the back room to look for her bag. The station was slow this morning; it didn't take long to sweep her eyes around the room and know her purse

wasn't there. Detective Andover was standing in the door of his office, talking with Jess's dad. They stopped talking when they saw her
approaching, a questioning look on Detective Andover's face.

"I'll follow up on this after court this morning," Jess's dad said,
waving the file folder he held in his hand. "Kelly." He nodded at Kelly
in a quick hello and walked toward the back of the station.

Kelly quickly told Detective Andover what she had returned for.
When her purse also wasn't where she had been sitting in his office,
he walked her back to the security door.

"Please, Miss Griffin, I know it can be hard to feel like you're doing nothing, but let us do our job."

"Have you found out anything about the toilet paper at our
house or the damage to our cars?" Kelly asked, glancing back to
where she had seen Jess's dad disappear. She and Wayne hadn't mentioned his ruse of having his friends tag another house to throw suspicion off of their house. Wayne's friends skirted the line sometimes
between a prank and arrest-able offense, and there was no reason to
throw them under the bus for trying to help.

"Actually, we may have," he said. "We're following up on a few
leads. I can't give you more information yet, as we're still investigating, but we are actively working on this. Just let us do our jobs."

Kelly had nodded, but she had her doubts. What sort of leads
did they have? Were they investigating both houses as the same
group of kids, or had they figured out they were separate incidents?
Should she have told him about Wayne's friends? Oh, man, she needed another cup of coffee!

She opened her eyes as she felt the truck slowing. Wayne was unbuckling his seat belt, already having grabbed the strap of his backpack. Dad was pulling up to the front of the school. Kelly knew
Dad would watch Wayne actually go into the building before pulling
away from the curb.

"Kelly, I wanted to talk to you alone," Dad said, glancing at her in his rearview mirror before hitting his directional to signal that he was pulling back into traffic. "I know you already know how much Wayne looks up to you. You've always been a good influence on him, which is one reason it was so hard to believe you let him come with you yesterday."

Kelly groaned. "Dad, I've said I'm sorry! You know I didn't try to get him into trouble, I was trying to help Sam!"

"I'm not just talking about going to Sam's apartment," Dad broke in. "I'm talking about the zombie party at your school. I know that with everything that has happened since then, it might seem like it's not that big a deal, but don't think we haven't been thinking about the kids that were brought to the hospital for alcohol poisoning. Did you know it was going to be that kind of party?"

Kelly opened her mouth, then closed it. Her shoulders slumped. "Well, I didn't know the drinking was going to get out of hand and the cops were going to be called, how could I? But did I know that there would be alcohol? Dad, it was a college party - of course there was going to be alcohol!"

Dad looked at her again in the mirror. He glanced at the road, quiet for a moment, then caught her eye again.

"You know the trouble that Wayne has been getting into. You know that he tends to follow others, and you know that he looks up to you. Surely you can see that bringing him to a party where you know there could be trouble is unwise?"

Kelly held her father's gaze. "Dad, I didn't drink. I wouldn't have let Wayne get into trouble. And I know Wayne is, well, Wayne - but he knows what you guys think about that kind of partying. He wouldn't have let himself get into trouble, either."

Her father looked back at the road. "Just, please, be aware of what kind of influence you are with him, that's all I'm asking," he said. He signaled to pull into the campus access road, pulling to a stop behind a line of cars trying to turn into the parking lot. "Which building are you going to?"

Kelly directed him to the library, planning to grab a coffee from the shop at the front before hitting her first class. Promising to keep in touch with her mother throughout the day, she climbed out of the truck. She struggled to pull her backpack free of the back seat, leaning in to slide its strap off where it had caught on the hinge of the front seat.

"I've got a couple of hours between classes, I might see if I can catch a ride back to the hospital if Rick is still there. I haven't heard from him since I saw him there on Monday," she said.

At her father's nod, Kelly shouldered her backpack and turned toward the library. As she joined the line at the counter of the cafe, she toyed with the decision of whether she wanted a caramel swirl or hazelnut coffee. If she was going to have to be Wayne's conscience as well as her own, she was going to have to increase her caffeine intake by at least half.

CHAPTER TWENTY-EIGHT

Kelly pulled the fabric at an angle and pinned it, cocking her head to one side and squinting her eyes to get a better idea of what the jacket would look like at a distance. The assignment was an easy one - tailoring a coat to fit a working class, middle-aged man with a paunch belly and flabby arms. The costume would be seen from a distance, and with stage lighting, so it didn't need to stand up to normal wear, but Kelly always turned in work that went above the professor's expectations.

"Tell me again, how do I attach this braid to the seam here?" Her classmate Erin asked, holding up gold braided ribbon and pointing to a pair of pants one of the cast members would wear during the marching band scene.

Kelly moved to the table and tucked in the end of the braid, showing Erin how to pin it so that she would be able to sew down the side without hitting the pins with the sewing machine needle.

"You're lucky your mom taught you to sew," Erin said, taking the pins and stabbing the braid where Kelly pointed. "My mother uses iron-on tape to fix hems. If a zipper breaks, she buys a new pair of pants."

Kelly laughed. "Honestly, so do I! I sew the fun stuff - I leave the fixing stuff for other people. Besides, some clothes are so cheap, you can't make them for what you can buy them for. But I agree, I am glad my mom taught me to sew. You're getting it, though - you can do the basics now, and some of the fun stuff. You'll see, it gets easier."

"Is this your first theater class?" Erin asked, pinning the rest of the braided ribbon and moving on to the other pant leg. "I was just taking the class as a good way to learn to sew, and add it to my syllabus, but I'm really loving it!"

"No, Kelly said. "This is my third year. I've taken the cosmetology class each year - its a basis for the theater makeup class. You can retake that one as many semesters as you want, and get credit each time, because you're helping on the productions and each semester is different, you know?" She moved back to the mannequin she had the jacket pinned on and began stitching a couple of basting stitches to hold things in place more accurately when she moved the jacket to the machine. "'The Music Man,' is cool, and I love getting to work on the costumes, but next semester will be 'Into the Woods,' and I can't wait to work on the make-up for that!"

Erin shook her head. "Not me. I have a hard enough time getting my eyebrows to come out even, I just can't imagine being able to make people look like real creatures just with make-up. I mean, in movies, at least they have computer graphics to add effects."

Kelly laughed. "I've been playing with Halloween make-up since I was a kid. I've gotten pretty good at gashes, zombies, that sort of thing - it doesn't really have to look alive, right? But I want to be able to transform someone to look not like themselves. You know, like Robin Williams in that 'Mrs. Doubt fire' movie. To be that good - that would be amazing!"

She had moved the jacket from the mannequin and placed it in the pile to be stitched on the machine. She picked up the next item on her table, a woman's blouse with puffy shoulders and neat white lace in a placket near the buttons. "See this shirt? For theater, you aren't going to really tailor this for the actress - you just have to get it good enough. It doesn't have to be exact, because maybe a different actress is going to wear it in the next show, right? Or they might use it for more than one scene, and it might need to fit differently. But prosthetic pieces made with latex and foam - the type of makeup that actors have to sit still while you apply it - that's not going to be just anyone who can do that. You have to be good. That's my goal."

Kelly heard shuffling and conversations escalating in volume and turned around. The class was ending, and most of the other students were packing up their things to head to their next classes. Erin noticed, too, and gathered up the pants to add to a pile of other clothing at the side of the room.

"I've got statistics in an hour, and I've got to reread the assignment. I'm sure I didn't get it right," Erin said, stuffing her tin of straight pins into her bag and swinging it over one shoulder. "See you next class."

Kelly nodded, gathering her own supplies, and smiled a goodbye. She had gotten distracted by the thought of the job she'd dreamed of since she was thirteen, to be able to work on a movie set and make fantasy creatures come alive. She glanced at the clock and swung the bag onto her shoulder. She didn't have another class for three hours. When she had seen her schedule at the beginning of the semester, she had thought it would give her too much time between classes, but she should have known better. There was never enough time in the day for her. She had begun spending extra time in between classes working on the costumes or hanging out with the make-up students, trying to pick their brains or just absorb by watching. There was also an enormous amount of work for her non-theater classes, but she usually managed to get that done quickly. Today, though, she was going to see Rick.

Kelly followed the sidewalk to the intersection near the parking lot, then meandered through the parked cars heading for the bus stop. She wasn't sure of the schedule but knew there were regular buses running the routes near the hospital. She'd catch one.

CHAPTER TWENTY-NINE

Rick was sitting up in bed, his leg outstretched under the sheets, his arms over his head with his hands laced behind his head. He was watching the TV mounted near the ceiling and didn't notice Kelly as she hesitated in the doorway.

"Hey, you look pretty comfortable there - what do you think, you're at a hotel?"

His head swiveled from the screen to look at Kelly. "Hey! 'Bout time you came back to see me!" He patted the bed and moved his legs over to give her a little room to sit down.

Kelly glanced around the room as she stepped inside, but didn't see a chair she could sit in instead. She sank down on the foot of the bed, holding her bag in her lap with both hands. "I wasn't sure you would still be here, actually," she said. "I thought you said you thought you were going to be one more day?" Her eyes followed the line from the IV bag and saw that it was still feeding into his hand.

"Yeah, turns out that some infections require a stronger antibiotic than you can take at home," he said. "I guess it's precautionary, but they wanted me to do at least 5 days of the IV stuff before I can start on pills."

"How's it feeling?" Kelly asked, glancing down at the leg but not touching it. Last time she had been in to see him, she had inadvertently increased his pain. She didn't want a repeat.

"Oh, you know, like I got knifed," he said, grinning at her. "No, seriously, it's sore as anything, but it could be worse. At least by my having to stay in the hospital for the antibiotic, my parents haven't gotten a chance to kill me, yet. They brought in my laptop so I could work on assignments, so I guess I still get to stay in classes. They did move me out of the dorm, though, and Mom had plenty to say about the shape of my room when they went in to get my stuff."

Kelly noticed the laptop laying closed on the bedside table. She moved her backpack to use it as a backrest and leaned back so that she could swing her legs up onto the bed beside Rick's. She had been a little nervous coming to see him, remembering how he had acted at the party, and in the hospital the next day. Rick was back to being Rick, though - funny, slightly spoiled, and comfortable to be around.

"My dad gave me a lecture this morning about looking out for Wayne," she said.

"Seriously? You weren't even there when the police crashed the party!" Rick was outraged on her behalf.

"Well, to be honest, he might have had a point," Kelly said with a grimace. She gave Rick the highlights of the events of the day before. "I wasn't thinking. I mean, I would probably do almost all of it again, but we should have told someone we were going. I'm still not sure if we should have told the police about the TPing or not. But I saw Jess's dad standing there, and he really has it in for Wayne. It just would have caused more grief. I'm sure my parents don't need that right now."

She realized she was trying to reassure herself more than explain anything to Rick. She shrugged, smiled, and glanced at the TV. "What are you watching?"

They passed the next 20 minutes picking apart the acting and costumes of the teens in the old horror movie he had been watching when she walked in before Kelly had to leave to get back to school for her last class of the day.

On the bus on the way back, she couldn't get past the feeling that there was something more she should do to try to stop the men who had attacked Sam. Digging through her backpack, she pulled out a sketch pad and pencil. She kept replaying her encounter with the man in the sweatshirt outside of the library. His face was so clear in her mind, she wondered if she could get a close enough likeness on paper. She glanced around the bus, but no one was sitting very close to her, and no one was looking at her. She started with a light touch, roughing in the basics, and was soon using a bolder stroke. She was so engrossed in getting the eyes right that she almost missed her stop. The bus rounded the corner and hit a pothole, jostling her against the side of the bus and making her look up. She grabbed her bag and fumbled it, her pencil and pad, and her cell phone as she stood and made her way to the door to disembark.

She took a few steps to the side to get out of the flow of pedestrians before putting her bag on the ground to put her things away. Holding up the sketchpad, she assessed the drawing with a critical eye. It wasn't great - but it might be close enough.

"Nice picture," the comment was thrown over a woman's shoulder as she hurried past. Kelly glanced around again, suddenly aware that she was crouched in the open holding a picture of a possible murderer. She stuffed the pad back into the bag pack and zipped it closed, then stood and swung it over her shoulder again. Her Sociology class was in the building to the left of the library, halfway across campus, and she had about five minutes to find a seat.

CHAPTER THIRTY

"They had to have been in there, I can't find the book anywhere!"

"Does anything look like it was touched? You said nothing in the house looked out of place," David said, his voice calm in opposition to the anxiety tightening his guts. He had tried to warn them, but it hadn't done much good.

"Nothing looks touched, but nothing looks the same, either." Mark was pacing around the car, running his hands through his hair. His eyes constantly swept the parking lot to make sure no one else was close enough to overhear them. Nervous energy poured off him.

"Dude, that makes no sense," David laughed, trying to lighten the mood. He turned away from Mark and ducked into the open car door, taking a deep breath as he leaned forward to grab his phone. He slowly breathed out, keeping his actions calm. He needed to make sure Mark couldn't sense his growing unease. He swiped across the phone to open the texting app and used the time to focus on slowing his breathing and calming his heart rate. Straightening from the car, he turned back to face Mark.

"Josh said there were a couple of bikes in the driveway, but he didn't see anyone inside, and he couldn't see anything amiss inside the house," David said. "If he hadn't said there were bikes in the driveway, would you have thought there was anything different in the house?"

David could see Mark mentally retracing his steps in the house. His face stilled. "The lights in Jill's bedroom. The lamp is on a timer so that it looks like there's still movement in there. It didn't go on last night - when I went in this morning, the wall switch was off. They were definitely in there. Shit!"

David shoved his phone into his pocket. He had tried to warn her, but he'd known when he saw her at the library he was too late.

He'd taken the chance when her brother called her name to get away, but he'd been worried that she wouldn't quit. He leaned back against the car and watched as Mark picked up his pacing again. He would have to be very careful if he was going to be able to keep the kids safe without blowing his own cover.

"I'm going to have to pay those kids a visit," Mark said. He leaned on his hands over the hood of the car, nodding to himself. "Stupid kids shouldn't be messing around with things that have nothing to do with them anyway. I need that book, and either Sam took it before she left, or they took it during their visit. If I don't make my deliveries, then people come looking for me, and I can't have that." He shook his head. "I knew that Sam was going to end up being trouble."

David didn't answer. He watched as Mark stared off toward the campus. He'd seen this side of Mark before, and as uncomfortable as some of his actions made David, nothing unnerved him like this side of Mark.

A car pulled off the street onto the access road and rolled toward the parking lot, bass speakers thumping. Mark's eyes narrowed as he followed it's progress. "This guy is late. If he doesn't have the money he owes me, he's going to wish he had called instead of coming in. I've got no patience for this today."

David watched as Mark straightened and stilled, eyes bright. He'd seen Mark like this when he thought he had been crossed. He hoped for the driver's sake, he had brought some money.

Mark tossed his head, shaking his shaggy hair out of his eyes. He braced his legs and crossed his arms over his chest. David knew Mark wouldn't walk over to the car, he would make the driver come to him. Ten seconds stretched into a minute. The heavy thumping from the car's speakers was beginning to grate on David's nerves. He glanced in at the driver, then quickly back at Mark. David wanted to see Mark's face, to see if there were any signs that would give away what might happen in the next few minutes.

The driver's door opened. The engine was still running, its radio still blaring its jarring racket, made louder with the opening of the door. A blonde girl with green streaks pieced into her hair closed the door quietly and strode confidently around the car to stand in front of Mark.

"Cory had an appointment he had to keep, but he asked me to bring you this," she said, wiggling one hand into the front pocket of the skin-tight jeans she wore and pulling out some wadded up money.

Mark stared at her, his face impassive. No muscles twitched at his jawline, no pulse beat at his temple. His eyes slowly scanned the girl's face, moved down to the bills in her hand, and back up to meet her eyes. The girl suddenly looked wary.

"Look, I'm just doing him a favor - he asked me if I had class today and could I come a few minutes early to see you and give you this money he owed you, and I said I would. He said he had to go to have a test done at the hospital, and it's one of those you have to have an appointment for - a cat scan? No, an MRI, I think, the one with the tube and the loud noise, and he was afraid to go because he's a big guy and he doesn't like tight spaces, and they gave him a prescription for something to relax him so he could go in the tube."

She was babbling. David was never sure how Mark was able to do it - he watched carefully, but had never seen anything that he could detect that would make people start spilling their guts, but they nearly all did. Mark would be utterly still, his eyes intelligent and interested, and something—something, but David couldn't figure it out - would cause people to bubble over with whatever Mark wanted to know.

Mark smiled, uncrossing his arms and reaching forward to touch the girl's shoulder. "Hey, I hope Cory is OK! He hadn't said he wasn't feeling well, I would have waited for the money. I mean, he knows I needed it back, my dad's been so sick and out of work so much, but

I could have figured something out." He was friendly and apologetic, his body relaxed.

The girl's smile lit up her face. David thought she looked relieved but knew if he were to talk to her later she would not remember feeling uneasy in the first place.

"Oh, he hasn't been sick! He said he was goofing around with his roommate and fell down the stairs. His shoulder's pretty messed up - that's why the MRI, to see if his rotator cuff is torn or something. Anyhow, he asked me to give you this, and said to say he'll catch up with you later."

She held out the money a second time. This time, Mark reached forward to take it. He smiled again.

David had seen that smile before, too. He closed his eyes, willing the girl to remember she had a class to get to. Apparently, it worked.

"Shall I tell him to call you, then? 'Cuz I've got to get to Dorsey Hall before class starts," she was moving toward the car. "I've got too many questions to get answers to about finding the outliers in statistics before the midterm next week!"

David watched Mark as Mark watched the girl drive Cory's car out of the lot and head for the back of campus. He met Mark's eyes as Mark turned from the car's taillights.

"I could use a new alibi," Mark said. One side of his mouth curled up slowly, but then his eyes hardened, and his jaw clenched. "First, though, I need to get that book back."

CHAPTER THIRTY-ONE

K elly slid her notebook out of her bag and showed the picture of the man in the sweatshirt to Sam.

"Do you know this person?"

Sam was sitting up in the hospital bed, leaning against the raised head of the bed. She looked at the picture, then reached out with one hand and took it from Kelly, slowly bringing it closer. She glanced up at Kelly and back at the pad in her hand. "This is David. Well, that's who it reminds me of - David has darker stubble, and his nose is a little wider, here, and something is different about his mouth - maybe David's is a little fuller? His jawline maybe a little wider?" She looked back at Kelly. "If this was just a picture you drew of someone, I would say you are an amazing artist - this is really fantastic. But this is too close to David to be coincidence, which means - did you see this guy while you were in Bridgeville? Oh, Kelly." The last was said in a near whisper. Sam looked close to tears. "Kelly, if David saw you, then Mark must know you were there. David is one of Mark's closest friends. This can't be good."

Kelly pursed her lips. Sam was looking and sounding so much better than she had last night, able to use complete sentences and thinking more clearly. Kelly realized she hadn't told Sam all of the details about the trip to Bridgeville. She didn't want to set Sam back since she was finally beginning to sound coherent, but she really wanted a way to make sure the family was safe again.

"Sam, help me make the picture more accurate. I wanted to bring it to the police station. If they have a picture of him, they'll have a better chance of finding him - and if they can find him, they can find Mark, right?" She gently pulled the sketch pad free of Sam's fingers. Digging into her backpack, she pulled out her case with pencils and a paper stump. "You think the jawline is wider, and the lips might be fuller?"

She moved the pencil over the surface of the paper, darkening here and there, rubbing with the stump on occasion and pulling out her kneaded rubber eraser to lighten or remove other details. She darkened the shadows on his chin and widened the nose. She agreed with Sam, this was looking more like the man she had seen in the halls of the hospital and following her in the library at Sam's school. The thought made her pause.

"Sam, he was here. I did run into him in Bridgeville, but first I saw him here, in the hospital," she said, her hand hovering over the picture. She looked into Sam's eyes. "I was in the chapel - it's on this floor. I had gone for coffee, and I saw a sign pointing the way to the chapel. While I was in there, I saw him walk past the door. I tried to follow him, but I lost him when I ran into a guy in scrubs coming around the corner. I told Dad, but I don't think he believed me. He said I couldn't be sure - there were other explanations for the things I had found, like a slip of paper with our address on it. But I'm sure it was him. He was here."

Sam closed her eyes and rested her head back on the pillow. Her voice was quiet. "When Jill first started going with Mark, they would hang out in the living room. I didn't much like him, so when they were over, I would study in my room, or go to work or the library. Jill had already changed - remember over the summer, I had told you that she had gotten quiet and looked like she wasn't eating enough, and she was sleeping a lot. I didn't like it, and when she started going with Mark she sort of got better, so I should have liked him, but there was something about him. I just got this feeling in my heart whenever he was around. And even though Jill was more outgoing and was eating again, she was just, I don't know, something wasn't right."

Kelly sat on the side of the bed, listening. Sam was picking at the edge of the blanket. Kelly noticed her fingernails were rough and jagged at the edges like they'd been chewed.

"David didn't hang out with them, but he would come around to talk with Mark at different times. I didn't get the same feeling that I did with Mark, that uneasiness, but when I walked through the room, I could feel their eyes on me. I started seeing him around town, at the bookstore, near my classes - I had never seen him in those places before so it couldn't have been a coincidence. He was following me - stalking me."

Kelly felt an iciness in her stomach. "Sam, did he - did he do anything to you?"

Sam shook her head, her eyes still closed. "No, that was part of what made it all so weird. He hardly even talked to me, and barely looked at me when I was in the room. He never touched me. He just was there, more and more, when I would turn around. And then, he was there when those, those things, took Jill." Her voice faded away as she pressed her lips together. A tear slid down one cheek from still closed lids.

Kelly reached out and grasped Sam's hand, squeezing it and holding on. "Sam," she said, not sure what else to add.

Sam opened her eyes. Misery pooled and spilled down her cheeks in hot tears.

"How could this have happened? Those things, how could they be real? And Jill! How could she be gone?"

Kelly dropped the sketch pad to the chair at the side of the bed and used both hands to pull Sam into a crushing hug. Wrapping her arms tightly around her older sister, she dropped her head onto Sam's shoulder and breathed a prayer that God would grant his peace because this was beyond her understanding.

• • • •

THE DOOR TO THE HOSPITAL room opened. Wayne walked in, backpack in hand, and reached to move the sketchpad so that he could sit in the chair. Glancing at the drawing, he looked up at Kelly, surprise evident in his open mouth.

"Kel, this is that guy! The one in the car with Mark! What did you draw him for?"

Sam drew back from Kelly's embrace, wiping the tears from her wet face with the hand without the IV.

"I wanted to give the police something to go on when they look for him," Kelly said, looking down at the drawing again.

Wayne was frowning, a small crease forming between his eyebrows. "I thought we were done," he said. "We gave the police the information we got from going to Sam's apartment. Dad said we need to let them do their jobs now." He lifted the sketchpad as though it was contaminated and thrust it back at Kelly. "You are going to keep at this, aren't you? You're going to keep pushing."

"What are you talking about?" Kelly raised her voice, stung. "How is my making a sketch - a sketch to give to the police, mind you - how is that not letting them do their jobs? How is that me keeping at this? And, really, why shouldn't we keep at this - if by keeping at this, you mean make sure the police keep working on it and trying to figure out who these people are and what is going on, and, more importantly, keeping us safe?"

Wayne was shaking his head. "No, Kelly. I know you. You push and push, and you become the distraction that derails things because you won't let other people do what they need to do. If you keep getting involved in their investigation, the cops are going to lose focus on what they need to focus on, and instead, they'll be focusing on you getting in the way all the time. Remember that time Gramma wanted to surprise Mom and Dad with a weekend away, and you kept trying to make everyone do things the way you thought they should be done, and in the end, Mom and Dad ended up with dinner and a movie?"

Kelly stood up, opening her book bag and putting the sketch pad back inside it. "Oh my word, Wayne, let it go. I did not push, and I am not going to be getting in the way of the cops doing their jobs. You sure weren't this concerned yesterday, when you called your buddies to throw the police off the trail. What I'm trying to do would actually help them!"

"Guys, stop it!" Sam was gripping the blanket in her hands, her head swiveling back and forth between the two of them. "Wayne, Kelly's sketch really could make a difference. I doubt I got any photos of David because he didn't hang around with Jill much. If I did, they wouldn't be close-ups. This picture is a good likeness. Why do you think it would be wrong to bring it to the police?"

Wayne shot a dirty look at Kelly's bag before turning back to Sam. "You were sleeping, so I'm not sure how much you heard about what happened while we were in Bridgeville the other day. Those guys threatened us - this guy didn't talk, but he was with Jill's boyfriend - Mark's the one who said something about my sister being gutted like a deer - so no, I think it would be better to just leave it with the police now!"

Sam's mouth dropped open as she turned to Kelly in disbelief. "You didn't tell me they threatened you! Kelly, maybe Wayne is right - I do think the sketch is good, and I don't see how it will hurt to bring it to the police, but we need to focus on staying safe. You drew David, which means you have probably been thinking about him all day, right? Kel, you know how you get - no, don't get mad, Wayne's right. You don't think straight when you're stuck on something. I don't want you getting hurt, too!"

Kelly ground her teeth. "I am not stuck on anything. I'm going to bring this sketch to the police, and then I'm going to head home to work on my sociology report. Can you stay here until Mom and Dad get back from dinner?"

She grabbed her backpack and swung it over her shoulder, knocking over a cup of water that had been sitting on the bedside table as she did so. "Crap!"

As she moved to grab a towel, Wayne waved her off, already having picked one up from a stack on the top of the built-in chest of drawers near the bathroom door.

"I've got it. You're like a wrecking ball with that thing," he said. "And I'll stay, but I'm not sure they'll be happy you went home without them."

"They're the ones who said we need to keep up with the workload. I'll be fine." She turned to look at Sam, who was watching her with a slight frown. "Really." Kelly turned more slowly this time and walked across the room to the door without knocking anything else over. She knew they were watching her. She refused to look back.

CHAPTER THIRTY-TWO

David turned his face to look at the trees flashing by on the side of the highway and mulled his options. He had offered yesterday to get the book by himself, but Mark was so beside himself with rage at Sam and her whole family that he wouldn't let go of the idea of watching their faces while he threatened them. He had agreed to have David accompany him there today, but David wasn't sure what good he was going to be able to do.

"That girl is going to be more trouble than her sister was," Mark said. He was tapping the steering wheel to the beat of a classic rock song, but clearly his mind was not on the lyrics. "Sam was quiet, and more moldable because of that. You weren't around a few years ago, but there was this girl, Amy. She was a treat, that one. She thought she was going to swoop in and stop me, like she was some sort of super hero coming to save the day. Ha! Should have seen her face when she saw what she was really up against! Ah, man, it was epic."

He tapped away on the steering wheel some more, smiling at the memory. David grinned and shifted in the passenger seat so that he partially faced Mark.

"OK, but seriously, what are we going to do when we get to Meldon? I think it might cause more problems if their whole family goes missing. Sam is in the hospital, the cops are looking into what happened. If the kids told the cops anything about coming to Bridgeville, it could be followed back to our backyard. That's just inviting unnecessary problems, in my opinion," David said.

"Nah, they can't go missing, you're right, there. I'm thinking of showing the little sister what sort of person I am. If she gets a good enough scare, and she finds out what could happen to Sam if I don't get what I want, she'll cooperate. She and the brother went to a lot of trouble to stick their noses in to try to defend their sister. That kind of person can be manipulated easily with the right leverage."

Mark drummed the steering wheel harder with the chorus. His grin returned. "Oh, man, I can't wait to see her face!"

"You think that changing in front of her and threatening her sister is going to dissuade her?" David was thinking of the determination he had glimpsed on Kelly's face when she grabbed his shirt outside the library the other day.

"Oh, that won't be a threat. Sam's going down whether I get the book back, or not. She should have kept her nose out of my business in the first place." Mark was serious now, the grin replaced by a stubborn scowl. "And her actually still being in the hospital is perfect for that part of the plan." He tapped the pocket of his leather jacket. "This stuff will mix right into whatever they've got in her IV, and send her right off the cliff. I don't have to kill her, I just have to ruin the rest of her life. Psych wards are filled with people who have come out the wrong side of a fight with my kind." The grin inched back into place on his face. "I'm actually looking forward to this. It's going to feel great to be able to stretch again."

David hit the lever to recline the back of his seat. "OK, wonderful, you get to scratch an itch, and we don't bring any trouble back home. We still have another hour or so before we get there, I'm going to relax." He closed his eyes and focused on slowing his heart rate. He would need to be doubly ready to turn things around if he saw an opening. To do that, he needed to make sure he gave nothing away before then.

Mark hung the nozzle back up at the side of the gas pump and flipped the gas cover closed. He knocked on the window to get David's attention, then pointed at the convenience store. David nodded and waved him off. He'd been thinking most of the ride down but was still not sure what to do. He expected he might not know until presented with an opening. He had to be ready to jump in when the time came.

The driver's door opened, and Mark slid in behind the wheel. He popped open a can of Mountain Dew and took a big swallow as he stuck the key into the ignition and cranked the car over. "You all caught up on your beauty sleep, Rip?"

David laughed as they merged back into traffic and mockingly stretched his arms as though awakening from a long nap. "Some of these classes are more involved than I thought they would be," he said. "I was up reading that book for my Risk Assessment class until three this morning - and then he didn't even bother to challenge half of the lame comparisons the class made. You would think that if the teacher is going to assign a book, he's already read it, right? But I don't think this guy has - or if he has, he has an earlier version with a different ending than the one I read last night."

David hadn't actually stayed up until three, and he'd had the book read since two days after seeing it on the syllabus. He also had been planning, not sleeping, but complaining about school was an easy out.

As expected, Mark laughed at the thought of an incompetent teacher. "Who's this, Mayhew? Hey, he's an easy grader - how do you think he keeps his job? Kids request him! They know he'll help them with their grade point average. He actually has pretty good contacts, though - he might suck as a professor, but he's pretty slick at knowing how to use his position to get what he wants. You should see his house."

David picked up his head and turned to look at Mark. "You've been to his house? He doesn't seem your type."

Mark managed to pull off an affronted look for about 15 seconds before bursting out laughing. "Well, I've seen his house - I never said I was invited! I've told you before, it makes good business sense to know what's being moved around you. He's got a nice little collection of African tribal masks displayed in a library at the back of his house. One of the dealers at a gallery in Boston told me she used to find them for him - apparently, he's worked his way up from simple costume masks to high-end collectibles. That kind of information can be handy to have, see?"

David gave a soft laugh, shaking his head. "Is there much that goes on in town that you don't know about?"

"Not much," agreed Mark, taking another slug of soda. "So, I've been thinking while you were snoozing over there. I've got to get that book back, and I've got to get these kids shut up, but these aren't my only problems. I've got a truck coming at the end of the week. I moved all the high-value items out of the house, but I'm going to need to find another place to keep them. Even once I get the book, I can't be sure the information hasn't been compromised, so I really can't keep using the house to shelf the inventory. That girl who showed up to pay down Cory's debt - she looked promising, don't you think?"

"That stringy blonde girl?" David injected a note of surprise and derision into his question. "You know, for someone with your experience with high-end merchandise, you sure seem to go for that lowest common denominator in women."

Mark laughed softly and threw a quick, questioning glance toward David.

"You have something bad to say about pretty much every girl on campus, Dave. Sometimes you make me wonder about you."

"Yeah, don't you worry about me. Apparently, I'm the only one with taste in this car, that's all." David knew that his celibate status would eventually raise Mark's suspicions, but he hadn't been able to make himself involve someone else in the case, even if it helped his cover. He had dropped hints at the beginning that there was a girl back home, hoping that Mark would think him just devoted - a trait Mark should value, even if he didn't share it. After the first year, though, it had been difficult to keep up the pretense, so Mark had fictitiously broken off the relationship. That had bought him some time as a lovelorn fool, but even that had not lasted.

"Seriously, what are you looking for in a woman that you can't find around here?" Mark persisted.

David groaned inwardly. He'd put Mark off when Mark had brought around women, hoping to set David up with one of them. Each time, he'd seen a calculating look in Mark's eyes. He knew that Mark wouldn't believe David had another out-of-town girlfriend, but he wasn't about to give Mark a chance to use another person as leverage to keep him in line. David had seen Mark exploit that subtle hypnotic power he seemed to have over other guy's girlfriends in a nearly effortless manipulation to accomplish what he wanted.

"Dude, I don't know. I don't have a 'type.' I like not having to answer to someone else, to sort my schedule around what someone else wants. I'm good the way things are, for now," he said.

Mark was shaking his head. "Nah, man, you need a woman. I'm going to make this my new mission, finding you a girl."

It sounded like a jest, but David knew that underlying Mark's joking tone was a very real intent. If this assignment continued, David was going to have to find a way to get Mark off his self-assigned mission or risk a genuine danger - for both David and whatever mystery woman Mark came up with.

Mark reached over and turned down the dial on the radio as he slowed down. They were coming up to the center of town now, and David knew Mark didn't want to draw undue attention. The sidewalks were not filled, as they had been over the weekend when David had come down with the others, following Sam, but they were busy enough.

"You said you remember the way to the hospital? I think we'll take a stroll through there, first," Mark said. He stopped at a crosswalk and motioned for a woman with a handful of envelopes to cross the street before moving forward. "It'll be easiest if she is still there. If she's already gotten out, we'll head over to their house."

David pointed at a sign on the light post, indicating the route to the hospital. He actually hoped Sam was still admitted, as it might keep the rest of her family safer. He wasn't sure if he would be able to tip off any of the hospital staff without tipping his hand, but it would be worth a try. They drove into the parking lot and stopped. David pointed in the general direction of Sam's room as they got out of the car.

"She's on the third floor if she's still here. I've got to hit the bathroom, though."

Mark was nodding. "I wouldn't mind that, either. And then I've got to find a supply closet."

David glanced over at Mark, careful not to change his expression. Mark was patting his jacket pocket, feeling with both hands as though to make sure everything he needed was in there. David had hoped for a couple of minutes to send a text message, but he couldn't do that if he couldn't get a couple of minutes away from Mark. They walked toward the building's entrance with David leading the way. Mark's glances took in the people in the foyer and vestibule. The bathroom was down a short hall from the vestibule but gave no privacy for David's message. He would have to figure something else out.

They moved to the elevator and rode up with a man holding a bouquet of yellow carnations artfully arranged in an oversized coffee cup. The doors slid open on the second floor, and the passengers all shuffled to the sides of the elevator to allow a couple holding paper bags filled with their lunches to board. The aroma of warm chicken and spices filled the small space. Mark turned his face toward the bags and inhaled deeply, eyes closed. David shook his head, smirking. Smells were a sure way to sidetrack Mark - too bad he hadn't had a burger or taco with him in the car when Mark started in about finding him a girlfriend.

The door slid open again on the third floor, and the couple stepped aside to allow David and Mark to exit. David glanced down the corridors in both directions. Seeing no one, he turned and began heading toward the wing he had watched Kelly enter when he had followed her the day after Sam had taken the bus home. Before they reached the hall, he turned into an intersecting hallway and pulled Mark to the side.

"The room she was in is just down there, but when I was here before they never left her alone. How do you want to play this? The kids are one thing, but both her parents have been hanging around, too," he said.

Mark turned his head to look back up the corridor they had been walking down, frowning thoughtfully.

"The kids have seen us, so they'll know who we are. The parents don't know us, though. If the parents are in there, but the kids aren't, they won't know I'm not the nurse I pretend to be. If the kids are in there, but the parents aren't, well, they just need to see what they're dealing with. If they're in there together, we'll go grab a cup of coffee and wait them out. I'm sure at some point, somebody is going to go home," he said. "So, now I need that supply closet. Why don't you stake out the room and see who is in there while I track down the clothes I need."

CHAPTER THIRTY-THREE

David watched until Mark disappeared around the corner. He stepped back to the hall he had been leading Mark down and took a few steps in the direction of Sam's room, just in case Mark was listening. He ducked into another doorway and, looking back down the corridor he had just walked, pulled out his cell phone. He quickly swiped in a message, hit send, and deleted the text from his history. Shoving the phone back into his pocket he stepped back into the hall and continued down the hall.

• • • •

DAVID EXAMINED THE notice on the board intently as the aide pushed past him with a cart of linens. He listened as her footsteps paused, a closet door opened, and he heard stacks of linens being transferred from the cart to the shelf. He made a pretense of moving on to another notice on the board, still intent on the sounds around him.

"I don't know, the primary care doctor diagnosed hantavirus, but I wouldn't be surprised if there was also leptospirosis in the blood – we won't know until further testing. That's one of the possible scenarios. We need to get the right antibacterial into her soon, or she might not recover," David heard a man's voice say as the door behind him opened and two sets of feet came into the hall.

David squinted at the notice and lifted his finger to trace a line of text. He had heard of leptospirosis before – where? He prodded at his mind, trying to remember. Something to do with a neighbor when he was younger. Aha – the man who had lived on the street behind him had been cleaning out a camper and cut himself while getting rid of a pile of mouse droppings he'd found in a cupboard. The bacteria in the mouse droppings had nearly killed him before he went into the doctor thinking he'd gotten a weird version of a summer flu.

David glanced back at the door, his expression deliberately vague. He had told Mark that Sam's room was down this wing, which it was - but on the fourth floor, not the third.

Fifteen minutes passed. David left his perusal of the bulletin board and took up a stance of patiently waiting outside the door of a room where he had seen the aides go in with a breakfast tray. If he looked like he was just waiting patiently, it would belay suspicion from anyone who had seen him lurking in the hall.

Mark finally came strolling down the hall, blue scrubs where his jeans and t-shirt had been, and a clipboard in his hands. He was reading from the clipboard and glancing at the room numbers as though looking for a specific patient. David cleared his throat quietly. Mark glanced at him, then at the room number on the wall near his head.

"This hers?"

David shook his head. He kept his face impassive. "Either she's been moved, or she's been discharged. There's an old guy with a bacterial infection in the room she was in."

Mark glanced around the hallway. Two nurses sat at the desk at the end of the hall tapping away on their computers.

"Didn't ask if she's still here?"

David shook his head. "Not yet, but I can. I'll meet you in the stairway."

Mark turned and sauntered back down the hallway. David stuffed his hands into his front pockets and moved to the nurse's desk.

"S'cuse me," he said, waiting until the young woman finished typing and glanced up at him. "I came in to visit my friend – I saw her earlier in the week here, I thought she was in room 308, but she isn't there. Can you tell me if she's been moved, or if she went home?"

The woman glanced around, her gaze taking in his t-shirt and unkempt hair along with the empty hallway behind him. Her lips softened as she smiled. "What's her name?"

"Sam – Samantha, Griffin."

Her fingers danced on the keyboard. "Oh, the girl with the bites." She looked up at David's face, her eyes suddenly hard. "She's been discharged. They were talking about several rehab facilities, not sure which one they ended up going with."

David's shoulders slumped, and he affected a disappointed expression. "Wow, I really hope she's ok. Thanks, I'll give her sister a call."

He turned to make his way back up the hallway to where Mark was waiting for him in the stairwell. The nurse's statement hadn't matched the expression in her eyes. She had almost looked angry, David thought, unnerved despite knowing the reason behind her change in demeanor. He glanced behind him and was not surprised to see her watching him. He continued on to the stairway, satisfied. This was working better than he had planned.

"She said the family brought her to a rehab, but she couldn't tell me which one – apparently they were looking into several," David said as he glanced up and down the stairwell. They were alone. "What's your plan?"

Mark was leaning with his back against the wall, one knee bent with the foot against the wall. He ran a hand through his hair and blew out his breath, tipping his face up to the ceiling. "I don't know, man. This would have been so much easier if Sam had just kept her nose out of things. What is it with this family? The sister and brother are the same way!"

He pushed off of the wall. "Come on. I'm going to get that book back. We'll find the sister. She wants to play investigator? We'll give her something to look for."

David had been thinking about this, had already considered that Mark would not give up just because Sam wasn't available. Still, he pressed to see if he could derail him from pursuing the book today. "Listen, Mark. You said you have orders to deliver. Let me track the sister down and get the book back. I can be back with it tomorrow or the next day, but you can still get your shipments made."

Mark laughed shortly. "Nah, man. I appreciate the offer, but I need the book to make the shipment – the details are all in the book. I mean, I remember all the items, but I'm not about to show up to deliver without reviewing the contracts- and making sure I have everything. No, I'm going to have to hang here, too, at least until we find her."

David shrugged. "Ok, just offering. Do you have a plan to find her?"

They had reached the foyer. Mark pushed the door open, shrugging his shoulders.

"Of sorts. We can do one of a few different things. We could go stake out their house and wait until she leaves, follow her, and pull her to the side where ever she ends up. We could stake out her school - I remember she said over the summer that she was going to the state school nearby, so she was commuting - there can't be that many state schools. The brother is still in high school - that's probably smaller, so he'd be easier to find, but we'd stick out more. Or," he opened the car door and swung into the driver's seat, "we just gatecrash the whole family at supper time and use them against each other as leverage. You can pick, I don't really care, but I'm getting that book back."

David's head whipped around as he lowered himself into the passenger seat. "Are you nuts? Gatecrash the whole family and take them hostage to use against each other? There's no way we'd get away with that!"

Mark shrugged his shoulders again, a menacing grin on his face. "I've still got the shot I was planning to give Sam - that would be enough to mess with their memories enough to throw suspicion off of us, I think. That, coupled with them getting a dose of what I can do, and I'm pretty sure we don't have to worry about them telling anyone. And if I'm not completely sure we'll be safe by the time we leave, well, then maybe they don't get a chance to talk."

David stared at Mark, then narrowed his eyes and turned to stare out the front window as though he was considering the option. He could feel the tension in Mark's posture. He knew he needed to calm himself before he spoke, or risk Mark's heightened senses picking up on his panic. Slowly, he breathed in and out, counting silently to five with each inhale and exhale.

"OK. Let's see if we can stake out the house, first, and see if she goes anywhere. If she's not there, we can try the school. I'd rather catch the sister than the brother, because, you're right - we'll blend better at the college. We've got several hours before supper time. Let's save that option for last case. Right?"

Mark was nodding in agreement, already turning the key in the ignition to crank over the car. David felt like he had passed a test of some sort. He drew in another breath and silently exhaled. Now he just needed to make sure they found Kelly before supper time. There was no way he wanted any part of a whole family of hostages and a vial full of Mark's voodoo magic.

They parked the car on the cross street and watched the house for ten minutes. Nothing moved. A car sat at the side of the house, but David knew that it hadn't been driven since the guys had trashed it the night they'd followed Sam home.

"Give me a few minutes, I'll see if there's anyone inside," David said, opening the car door before Mark could object.

There was no point in staking out the house if there was no one home, and David would rather use the time finding Kelly rather than watching an empty house. He strolled down the street toward the house, nodding his head as though to music in his head as he glanced at other houses on the road. It looked like there were a few kids in the backyard in the house at the end of the street, but he couldn't see anyone in the yards or windows of the homes closer to the Griffin's house. He chanced a glance behind him toward Mark in the car, then walked up the driveway toward the house. As he flitted a look toward the houses on either side of the Griffin's, he stepped off the driveway and took a step toward the first-floor window. No one. He walked to the next window - again, no one. Glancing back to Mark's car again, he took a deep breath and rounded the corner to check the windows on the side and back of the house.

"Not home," he said, as he opened the car door and dropped into the seat again.

"Want to give it a few minutes?" Mark asked idly. He was tapping to the beat of a song on the radio, his head relaxed against the headrest on his seat.

David sensed the test rearing its head again. He paused, then shrugged.

"Your call. I think we'd spend the time better checking at the school, but you're the one driving this bus," he said.

Mark's head bobbed forward and back, then side to side to the beat. Finally, he nodded and turned the key again. "Yeah, you're right. Besides, I want something to eat. The cafeteria's probably got cheaper food than anywhere else."

David pulled the shoulder strap down to buckle the seat belt around his waist and tapped his hand on the car door near the window. If things were going his way, they'd run into Kelly and be able to quickly and smoothly convince her to turn over the book to them. If possible, he might even be able to talk to her without Mark right there and convince her to just go with his suggestions to keep her family safe. Things were so close to being closed down, it could jeopardize years' worth of tenuous and fragile inroads if Kelly balked. David pulled out his cell phone and opened his GPS. Searching for colleges, he located a community college to the west and a state college to the north.

"You've got about 20 minutes before lunch," he said, cranking up the volume on the phone's media player and putting the phone in the cup holder between the two seats.

CHAPTER THIRTY-FOUR

Kelly stood and slid her sewing kit into her bag as the rest of her classmates filed toward the door. She'd been tacking a hem and hadn't noticed the time until the professor announced midterm projects would be due in another week. She joined the end of the line to exit the classroom, then headed for the bathroom. She'd been living on coffee and coffee for the past couple of days, which meant frequent trips to the bathroom. It wasn't doing much for her nerves, either, she acknowledged to herself.

After a quick trip through the bathroom, Kelly glanced at her watch. Nearly lunchtime. She wasn't really hungry, but she knew she should grab something. Maybe a cup of soup would be comforting - and better for her than another cup of coffee. Slinging her bag over one shoulder, she made her way out of the building and headed across campus to the student government building. She glanced at the windows of the bookstore as she passed. The reflected version of herself looking back at her looked harried. Kelly knew the dark surface of the tinted window gave a sharper edge to the shadows on her face, but still, she grimaced at her reflection and turned her face resolutely away. Mid-terms, Sam, and trying to keep her mind focused while all the while, at the edges of her thoughts, nibbled the ideas of shapeshifters and drug users and smugglers of various wares - she was having trouble sleeping, as well as eating.

The smell of lasagna and fresh bread baking scented the air as soon as she walked through the cafeteria doors. Kelly lifted her nose in appreciation. Maybe she would be able to stomach something for lunch after all. She turned toward the line, then surveyed the tables. She saw Maria, a girl she had worked with on a few projects in psychology class, with an empty seat beside her. Kelly lifted one hand in greeting, then froze. Rising from a table just behind Maria, staring at Kelly with a cold, hard stare, was Mark.

176

Kelly took a couple of steps backward, then turned and jostled through the students who had joined the line behind her.

"Geez, make up your mind - you getting food or not?"

Kelly apologized, pushing blindly through. What was he doing here? He had clearly seen her, and recognized her - what should she do? She knew he was here for her - why else would he be here? Panic rose in her throat, threatening to choke her. She reached the sidewalk in front of the building and stared wildly around. Where? Where? She stumbled up the stairs of the building next door. Dashing into the hallway, she saw a few students clustered around a poster on the wall. She murmured another, "excuse me," as she barreled past. The hallway opened into a foyer with stairways opening off of two sides. Kelly grabbed the railing and whipped around the newel post, taking the stairs two at a time. She needed to get away - but she needed to know if he was following her. Her blood was pounding in her temples, her hands trembling as they grabbed the railing and helped her to keep from tumbling.

At the top of the stairs, she darted to the right, taking the corridor above the hallway she had just come down. There was an open study area at the end of the hall - she could look out the windows there to see what was going on outside. As she neared the end of the hall, Kelly risked a glance back toward the stairs. A couple of students stood watching her, naturally curious as to her quick steps, but no one was chasing her. She slowed, trying to catch her breath.

Kelly stepped to the side once she reached the study area. The hall basically opened into the large, open space. A few stuffed chairs were spaced out with some tables and chairs clustered here and there. Kelly glanced around. The two girls in the area were sitting at one of the tables discussing a video they were watching on a laptop. Glancing back over her shoulder toward the stairs, Kelly walked across the open area to the windows. She stood to one side and peeked out around the curtain, not wanting to be seen from below. She didn't see him. Campus wasn't too busy - people were milling about, but not so many that she would be unable to spot him if he was there, which meant one of two things. Either he hadn't followed her, and was actually not there to try to get to her, or he had followed her, had seen her enter the building, and was already inside, where she couldn't see him.

She darted another glance back at the stairway and froze. Mark was walking toward her, with the guy Sam had called David. Kelly glanced at the two girls with the laptop. They were laughing over something that was happening on their video, oblivious to the fact that Kelly was standing behind them, never mind that two men were ready to inflict heavy damage on her. She looked back at Mark. He wasn't even breathing hard. He walked calmly across the study area until he was close enough to reach out and touch her, then stopped. David stood just to his side, partially turned so that he could see the girls at the table. His face was impassive, his hands tucked into his pockets in a loose way that should have been friendly but made Kelly very aware of her shortcomings.

"How is Sam?" Mark asked, a note of concern in his voice. "We stopped at the hospital to see her, but they said she had already been discharged, to a rehab - shame how many kids these days are turning to drugs, isn't it?" The concern had disappeared from his voice, leaving it taunting and dangerous.

Kelly tightened her grip on the strap of her backpack, glancing again at the girls watching their video. Surely they would look up, would see she was in trouble! Mark's gaze followed hers.

"Let's take a walk, hey?" he said softly.

Kelly shook her head and tried to back away, but her backpack bumped against the wall behind her. "I'm not going anywhere with you," she bit out. Anger and fear warred in her head and made her voice shake.

Mark stepped closer. He put one hand on her arm and squeezed. Kelly felt hot pain in her arm and glanced down, alarmed. The fingers on the hand Mark gripped her with looked strange - twisted, with long, sharp nails he was digging into her. In the seconds she watched, dark hairs grew on the back of his hand. Her eyes flew back to his face, which wore a satisfied smirk. "You will come with me unless you want a lot more people to get hurt," he said.

"Hey! Are you okay?"

The girls with the video had finally noticed that they were in the room. Kelly glanced back over at them. The girls were looking at Kelly pointedly, their expressions supportive. Mark's fingers squeezed Kelly's arm again. If she tried to get away from him, what would happen? What would he do to these girls? What could he do to them - what was he? Suddenly his hand was gone from her arm.

"Sorry!" Mark's hands were in the air, palms open, and he wore a sheepish grin. "Didn't mean to startle her, but I guess I did! Her sister's a friend of mine, and we just found out she's been sick. I guess my showing up to ask about Sam wasn't expected, that's all."

Kelly stared at him in shock. He was clearly insane. She glanced at his hands again and froze. His hands looked normal - fingers straight, nails short. She turned back to the girls and was shocked to see them smiling understandingly at Mark and turning back to their video. She faced him again, eyes narrowed. David still stood beside him, his gaze on Kelly steady. Mark lowered his hands as the girls turned away, then shifted his focus back to Kelly.

"That walk, shall we?" he said. "David here has made me promise you won't get hurt so long as you help us out." He nodded toward David, who gave no indication of hearing him.

Kelly's hands tightened again on her shoulder strap. She was backed in a corner here, but at least she was visible. If she moved two steps to the right, she'd be in full view of anyone looking up from outside. If she went with these guys, she had no belief that she would escape unharmed.

It was as though Mark could see her thoughts cross her face. "If you don't come with me, I can make sure those girls never forget this afternoon. How long do you think it would take someone looking up from outside to figure out something horrific was going on in here - five minutes? Ten minutes? And how long before they would be able to get up here to try to stop it - another minute or two? It took my friends less than five minutes with Sam at the bus stop, and she had an idea of what she was dealing with. What do you think I could do to these girls in 12 minutes, when they think I'm just a friend looking for information about your sister?"

His quiet intensity was more sinister than Kelly wanted to acknowledge. Glancing back at the girls, she gave a small nod.

CHAPTER THIRTY-FIVE

Kelly drew back from Mark's hand on her arm again, but at his tug, she took a step toward him. He smiled toward the girls at their table as he put his arm around Kelly's shoulders. Her skin crawled and she stiffened, but she took another slow step alongside him as he led her out of the study area. David fell into step just behind her.

Kelly walked stiffly. When they were away from the girls, she shrugged Mark's arm off her shoulders.

"Enough. What do you want?" She demanded, crossing her arms in front of her and lifting her chin.

Mark glanced around. Grabbing her arm again, he tugged her into an empty classroom and closed the door behind them. Apparently satisfied they would remain undisturbed, he returned his gaze to her face. His mouth twisted into a sneer, and then something more. His jaw seemed to jut forward, lengthening, and short hairs sprouted so quickly along it that his beard rapidly covered most of his face. His teeth snapped twice, his tongue flicking in and out of his mouth.

Kelly's limbs were frozen, her eyes wide in horror. She opened her mouth to scream, but David's hand covered her mouth, his body a solid wall at her back. His other arm slid around her waist and squeezed. "Shh. Hear us out," she heard his whisper at her ear.

Mark's face was sliding back into that of a man. Kelly could feel her body trembling, her muscles tight and unwilling to listen to her brain as it screamed at them to move. Mark smirked as his jaw returned to its familiar shape. She could see his enjoyment at her fear. Somehow the laughter in his eyes made her angry - and that gave her strength. She grabbed at David's hand at her mouth and worked to separate his pinky finger from the rest, kicking back with her heel to stomp on his foot. She pulled at his finger and managed to twist so that his hand came free of her face.

181

"Let go of me!" she demanded, jabbing backward with her elbow. She heard his gasp as she landed her jab and his grasp around her waist slackened. She took one step, then froze. Where Mark had stood smirking now crouched a fur-covered dog baring its teeth. A low growl rumbled from its chest. Kelly scrambled backward, running into the wall of David's body again. His arm wrapped tightly around her waist again.

"Stand still!" he hissed.

She froze, her chest barely moving with her shallow breaths. The dog took two menacing steps toward her, a low and deep growl emanating from between its bared teeth. Kelly shrunk backward into David's grasp, her eyes squeezed shut - sure the animal was about to rip her to shreds. Instead, she heard a breathless laugh. Opening her eyes, she saw Mark standing just inches away from her, and shoved him away with both hands. Opening his mouth in a snarl, he lunged back toward her with a roar.

"Stop!"

It was David, one arm still tightly gripping her around the middle, the other pushing Mark's chest away. Kelly felt herself pulled off balance as David wrenched her to the side, stepping forward to confront Mark.

"You've shown her. It's enough." He bit out to Mark. Turning his face toward Kelly, he shot, "Stop! Don't you learn?"

Kelly's fingers gripped his forearm as she tried to regain her footing. Her legs were shaking so badly she was afraid they wouldn't support her weight. As she stared wildly back toward Mark, she saw him laughing again.

"It's all good, you can let her go," he said, walking to sit on the corner of a table. His posture was relaxed, but Kelly saw that he had positioned himself between her and the door.

"Do you want to sit down?" David's hands were righting and steadying her, his words quiet and calm.

Kelly shook her head, unwilling to look away from Mark. She struggled to form a coherent sentence. "What are you?"

Mark threw back his head and laughed. "Right now, sweetheart, you can consider me your worst nightmare. I'm someone you don't want to mess with - got that?"

Kelly gave a small nod.

"Now. You or your sister took a book from the apartment that I need back. You are going to get it for me. I don't think I need to tell you what I will do if you refuse to help me, but I want to tell you. I don't want you to have any misgivings. You get me the book, or I will visit your brother, your mother, your father - do you understand?"

His expression hardened as he stared at her. Kelly swallowed and quickly nodded again as she realized he was waiting for a response.

He nodded in approval. "Good. The book is a maroon notebook. There are some papers stuck inside - they'd better still be there when you bring me the book. I'm going to give you, what, a day?" He looked at David, eyebrow lifted.

Kelly felt, rather than saw, David nod.

"Do you need eyes?" David's question was directed to Mark.

He pursed his lips, considering, then nodded. "Yeah, that's not a bad idea. I have an appointment tonight, but I can be back tomorrow afternoon to pick you up." His eyes found Kelly's again. This time, there was no mirth in them. "You find that book. You have until tomorrow - you find it, David will give me a call. If you don't, well, it wasn't difficult to track you down. It won't be hard to find the rest of your family. I've got a pretty good nose for sniffing out problems." His grin was back, though it didn't reach his eyes.

In one fluid movement, Mark was on his feet. He motioned with his head, and David followed him into the hall and closed the door to the classroom behind them.

Kelly looked around the classroom dazedly, then sank into one of the chairs. She put her hand up to her forehead as a wave of dizziness swept over her. Opening her eyes and looking around wildly, she bolted out of the chair and made it to the trashcan near the teacher's desk before getting sick. She wretched until there was nothing left of her breakfast. Pushing her hair away from her face, she sat back and leaned against the desk with her eyes closed, tears escaping from beneath her lashes.

CHAPTER THIRTY-SIX

"Here."

Something cold and wet touched her face, and she jumped, eyes flying open. David was crouched in front of her, a wet paper towel extended toward her in one hand. Kelly groaned and pushed his hand away. He withdrew the paper towel, but didn't move away. Kelly looked at him completely, for the first time since she had seen him next to Mark. The sketch she had done of him had been very close, though Sam had been right - his nose was a little wider than she had drawn it, and his lips a little fuller. She had also missed a small scar on his left cheek.

"So, what are you, my guard dog or something?"

He shook his head. "I'm not one of them. I'm actually, well, I guess I am a guard dog of sorts - a guard dog is supposed to protect, and that's my goal. Listen, do you feel well enough to stand? This would be easier for you if you were walking."

Kelly raised her eyebrows at him. "That doesn't make any sense," she said, but she struggled to get to her feet. The smell from the trash can was threatening to make her sick again. She ignored David's extended hand and pulled herself up so she was propped on the edge of the desk.

David sighed, leaning back on one of the nearby desks. "Look, I know you don't trust me, and you have no reason to. I have answers, though. I can help you, and I think you can help me. Would you at least hear me out?"

Kelly reached out a hand toward the wet towel he still held. When he handed it to her, she used it to wipe her face off before tossing it on the top of the vomit in the trash can. Wordlessly she straightened from the desk, reached down to grab her backpack, and walked to the door. She turned to see him watching her from his spot near the trash can. Tipping her head, she waited until he took a few steps toward her before opening the door and walking out of the room. He matched her stride as she headed for the end of the building away from the cafeteria.

"Where did he go?"

"Back up to Bridgeville. He said he's got deliveries to make."

Kelly glanced at him as they took the stairs to the first floor. She stayed silent as they wound their way through a crowd in the vestibule, then pushed the door open and stepped out on the sidewalk. Kelly's eyes swept the campus quickly as she headed for the bus stop. Halfway across campus, though, she stopped. Turning to face David, she waited.

"He's a werecoyote."

Kelly stared at him. She wanted to accuse him of thinking she was an idiot, of lying to her, but she could think of no plausible explanation for what she had just seen.

"Never heard of those," she finally said, looking around campus again.

He nodded. "Most people think werewolf, but those are actually bigger and less accommodating."

Kelly shot him a glance to see if he was being sarcastic. To his credit, he was keeping a straight face. He continued looking steadily into her face. "Werecoyote are cunning and sneaky. They are more in control of their actions when they change than werewolves are. You saw Mark - as a werecoyote, he can control how much he changes, and when. He keeps greater control of his urges, so to speak, when he does change. A werewolf would likely not have been able to only show you a peek, and once changed, would react as an animal if provoked." He rattled off the information like Wayne comparing hood scoops or manifolds when he was thinking about changing something on his car.

"What do you change into?" Kelly asked boldly.

David was shaking his head. "I told you, I'm not one of them. I don't change into anything - what you see is what you get."

"Hmph. So, sneaky, drug dealing fan-boy it is, huh?" Kelly almost regretted the words as soon as they were out of her mouth, but none of this felt real to her. If she woke up and realized this had all been a dream, and she had allowed herself to be manipulated and patronized and hadn't even tried to stand up for herself, she would be horrified.

David was shaking his head again. "OK, maybe I worded that poorly. What you see is not exactly what you get, but I don't change into anything - think of me as wearing a disguise. It's taken me three years to get where I am in Mark's organization, and I've only gotten this close because of my disguise. We're at an impasse, though, and I could use your help."

Kelly surveyed his features skeptically. "Right. You're some kind of undercover myth hunter, you've been working on this for years, and all of a sudden I'm the one who can help you? Not buying it, sorry. Come up with a better cover story, see if I bite." She crossed her arms in front of her chest and braced her legs. "Go 'head. But hurry it up, because I'm getting cold." She was getting cold. A wave of shivers crossed her shoulders, and she tightened her crossed arms.

David was looking across campus, shaking his head at her attitude. "Listen, is there a library we can go to? The one on our campus has study rooms - I imagine most do. We could use one of those - it'd be warm, it's open, so you'd know you were safe, and it's private, so we know no one will overhear what we have to say. No, wait," he put up one hand in the air, palm side toward her, as she made a motion to leave him standing there. "Mark will come looking for your family, Kelly. He wasn't bluffing. You're going to have to give him the book. If I can't convince you to work with me, I still have to keep an eye on you - there's so much more riding on this!" He ran a hand through his hair, leaving it sticking out in strange places. "Could we just go to the library and talk?"

Kelly sighed, then shivered again. Nodding once, she grabbed the straps of her backpack and altered her course toward the library.

CHAPTER THIRTY-SEVEN

"So you're an undercover cop? Show me a badge," Kelly said. They were sitting with the table between them, safely ensconced in one of the private study rooms in the history section.

David rolled his eyes. "If I was an undercover cop, how stupid would I be to carry a badge on my person?" He asked. "But no, I'm not a cop. I work for a quasi-governmental taskforce. We're like a black ops unit - meaning that there is no official recognition of the taskforce and no recognition of me as an agent at all. Yes, I know, this sounds far-fetched and like I'm trying to pull a terrible joke over on you. I'm not. Just let me explain."

He was leaning forward over the table, one arm stretched forward as if to pull understanding out of her. She had pushed her chair back from the table as far as it would go and sat stiffly, her arms crossed in front of her. She felt tightly strung, suspicious of every muscle twitch, every raised eyebrow of every person they had passed on the way to this room.

"Yes, it does sound like some far-fetched story from the Twilight Zone or something. I don't happen to like the Twilight Zone, by the way. Why don't you just cut to the chase?"

David leaned back in his chair, considering her. He shook his head.

"No, you really need me to start at the beginning. You need to understand. I need you to understand - because you need that in order to be willing to work with me," he said. "Just, listen. Take a deep breath, and listen."

For the next half hour, Kelly listened. She was skeptical, then horrified, disgusted, and finally, willing to give David the benefit of the doubt - doubt she still carried, in spades.

"If you're sure he's part of this smuggling ring, why haven't you moved in before now? Why wait until Jill and Sam got hurt?"

189

"He's definitely part of the smuggling ring. The problem is that the deeper I get in his organization, the bigger I find that the ring is. Shifters like Mark are called shades, because they operate just at the edge of society, using their skill-sets to blend, like shadows. They're hard to police; some are more difficult than others. Initially, we thought it was drugs, and then we found out about the peyote and other cactus strains. Mark's gotten very good at using the cactus on other people, and making concoctions that give 'trips' without nausea. He uses the cactus as a way to control the people around him. Then I found out about the bears. I don't think he even really believes in them possessing any real medicinal value - he's just in it for the money, and the thrill of being a player on the black market. From comments he's made, though, I think he's got an even more valuable commodity he's been trading," David had been watching the library beyond the study room through the windows as he spoke. Now he looked directly into Kelly's eyes. "Jill isn't dead, Kelly. I know that Sam thought she was - two of the coyotes smelled Sam's presence when they were bringing Jill to the warehouse. Mark had miscalculated how much K it would take to make her compliant, and he knocked her out. He was turning her over."

Ice had entered Kelly's veins. "What - what do you mean?" She whispered, horror-struck. "You mean, like a prostitute?"

David was running his hands through his hair again, his elbows on the table. "I don't know what they end up being used for - but yes, I mean he's trafficking humans. He's selective. He hasn't taken too many from campus - I think he's gotten a couple there, but he's gotten more from cities nearby. I've seen a few of them, and then we don't see them anymore. I've heard a few comments that make me think he's selling them."

Kelly opened her mouth to speak, then closed it. She began again. "And your plan is for me to help you - help you with what? I'm not going to -"

"No! No," David cut her off before she could finish her protest. "I absolutely am not asking you to put yourself in any more harm's way than you already have," he assured her. "But you have to realize - you already are in danger. You put yourself there when you went to Sam's apartment. Mark is not going to forget that you have seen his products, and, probably even more importantly, you either have or will have the book. He's going to believe that you will read it, right? He wouldn't send anyone to get it, he made sure he came for it himself, and I've been expressly directed to call as soon as you find it. He was acting too casual about it, which leads me to believe that he's concerned I will look at it, but afraid that if he tells me not to, it will make it more like forbidden fruit."

David shoved his chair back and began pacing on his side of the table. He glanced around the room beyond the window again, and then back at Kelly. "I have to tell you, I don't have a good feeling about this. I'm not a coyote, but I've lived with them and worked with them long enough to know a bit. Mark needs you to get the book, but I don't think he's going to leave it at that."

"Why am I not going to the police, then? I could just turn the stupid book over to them - let them deal with him!" Kelly's thoughts were slamming around in her head - she couldn't think straight. What was she supposed to do? How could she keep her family safe?

David shook his head. "If we were just dealing with a drug dealer or even a smuggler, I would agree with you - but I wouldn't even be here if that's all we were dealing with. Mark's a werecoyote. How are you going to explain that to your police? Who's going to believe you? And Mark has this, well, I don't know exactly what it is, but he has this charm that can completely take people in. You saw a little of it, with those girls in the room where we found you. Say he decides to turn that on, and they let him go? What do you really have on him?"

"I have his stinking book!" Kelly's voice rose as she struggled to control her panic. "Oh, God, help me," she murmured. She jumped to her feet - she just couldn't sit still anymore.

In two steps, David was at the end of the table near the door, neatly preventing her escape. "What do you mean, you have his book? You already know where it is?"

CHAPTER THIRTY-EIGHT

K elly gave a shrill laugh, barely restraining her panic. "I know exactly where it is - Sam didn't take it, I did! I didn't know it was his; I thought it was just Jill's diary. I was looking for answers for what happened to Jill, and maybe what happened to Sam. Oh, my God," she muttered the last sentence into her hands as she squeezed her temples. "What have I done?"

A curious expression flitted over David's face and was gone. He shrugged his shoulders and pulled his own chair back up to the table. "I've got an idea. We've got to get Mark's book back to him, and then convince him that you and Sam are dead. It's the only way he's going to let this go. If he thinks you two were the only ones to see it, he'll leave the rest of your family alone. He thinks Sam took it, and that you're going to find it and give it back, so there is no way to not include the two of you. With all the trouble Sam caused, he's not going to let her get away, anyway."

Kelly was stunned. The situation was getting stranger and scarier with every minute that ticked past, but she was mired in shock. "How are we going to convince him that Sam and I are dead? Sam is still at the hospital. Mom and Dad were thinking of taking her to our aunt's house, but the hospital wanted another day of observation. She had a reaction to the anesthesia because of whatever he'd been dosing her with - a serotonin overdose, the doctor said. He could have really killed her!"

David was nodding. "Mark thinks Sam is already at a drug rehab about an hour away. That buys us a little time, but probably not enough. Shoot," Mark rubbed his forehead again, "I wish we could have had this conversation before Mark got to the hospital. I had to act quickly - he had a syringe, probably of his 'cactus juice,' he was going to inject into her I.V. I sent a quick text because it's all I had time for. We were already in the building." He shook his head, lifting his chin a fraction. "Well, it bought us time. If he had found her at the hospital, she would be dead, and we wouldn't get the chance to figure out a way to fake it."

"I don't understand," Kelly said. "What do you mean, you made a quick text? Who did you text? How could you hide her?"

"I sent word to a guy in my unit to call the nurse's station. He told them he was with the police, and that they had reason to suspect her dealer was trying to find her. They have protocols in place to take care of at-risk patients. He asked them to use them. So, when we showed up a few minutes later, asking about her, they told us she had already left the building, and suggested she might be at a facility a distance away. In actuality, she's still in the same room. I had to tell Mark I knew which room was hers, but I stood outside some other patient's room to throw Mark off." He lifted one shoulder in a half-shrug. "If Mark had really wanted to test me, he would have gone into the room to see who was in there, or he would have asked the nurse at the desk where Sam was himself. It was risky, but I needed to know he still trusted me, too. It's the only way this plan has half a chance of succeeding."

Kelly tried to think logically, but the underlying panic thrumming through her body kept her mind spinning fruitlessly.

"This isn't possible. None of this makes sense," she muttered, closing her eyes. Opening them again, she found David looking at her sympathetically. She took a deep breath and blew it out slowly.

"That's good," David said, nodding. "Deep breathing helps. You can try to focus on calming your heart rate, too. Don't think about the chaos around you, just the slow, steady beat." He waited, watching as she closed her eyes and took another breath. "I know this is a lot to take in, Kelly. I know I'm asking a lot of you, but it's the only way I can think of that will get you and your family out of Mark's path. As it is, I don't have all the details worked out, yet."

Kelly focused her mind on the image of the storm she had seen on the Facebook meme on the bus ride home the other day, silently repeating the verse that had been with it. She opened her eyes again. "You said you're part of a government agency. If we can't go to the police because of his charm, or whatever it is, why can't we go to your agency? Shouldn't your guys be able to protect my family?"

David sighed. "My team is small. When we do move on him, and we were getting close to that point, but we weren't there yet, it will be to manage the whole ring, not just Mark's cut of it. If we expose our hand too early, which interfering to protect your family would do, we lose more than just Mark and his pack - we lose the whole ring, and they double down on their efforts to hide their trail. I wish there was another way to do this, I do, but it's not just your family at stake here. Imagine the chaos going on with your family multiplied by hundreds - that's the size of what's at stake." David looked at her closely. "Kelly, I know that Sam is a Christian - I've heard her mention her Bible study and I have seen her prayer lists at the apartment. I'm not saying this to manipulate you - but if you are a believer, too, then you must know that God sometimes puts people into situations to stretch them. I'm not saying this is that, exactly. I'm just, I don't know - asking you to trust him, even if you don't trust me."

Kelly stared into David's face, trying to see if his sincerity was genuine. She licked her lips, aware of the taste of sour vomit. Glancing at the clock in the main library, she saw that it had been less than three hours since she'd first seen Mark in the cafeteria. "Tell me your plan."

CHAPTER THIRTY-NINE

"**N**o. Absolutely not."

"Sam, we don't really have a choice!"

"Kelly! There has to be another way - you can't get that close to him again!"

Sam was sitting in the chair near the window, wrapped in her bathrobe. She still had the IV lines taped to her hand, though they weren't connected to the IV at the moment. When Kelly had walked into the room, she'd gestured at David to stay in the hallway and let her talk to Sam first, but he'd shaken his head and followed closely on her heels. Sam had glanced up, then jumped backward in the chair and grabbed for the call light cord. Kelly had rushed forward to catch her hands and hugged her tightly, repeating over and over that she was OK, that everything was going to be OK, until Sam stopped fighting her and calmed enough to listen to them. David had moved the call light cord far enough away so that Sam couldn't reach it, then backed up and stood quietly against the wall where Sam could see him easily.

"Sam. You've seen enough of what Mark can do," he said now. "He is coming for you, and he's coming for Kelly. The best way that I know to keep you safe is to try this."

Sam had refused to do more than cast furtive glances in David's direction while Kelly had laid out the plan. Now she lifted her chin a fraction as she stared accusingly at him. "To keep us safe? You? You were there the whole time he was poisoning me! You were there when he killed Jill! You don't care about keeping us safe!"

"Jill is not dead," David said. "At least, I'm fairly certain she isn't. In any case, Mark didn't kill her. He dosed her with drugs - I'm not saying he's a nice guy!" David was holding up his hand to stop Sam from interrupting him. "I'm just saying that he didn't kill her."

Sam sat upright in the chair. "But, I saw him! I saw him, and those, those things, that were dragging her on the ground - I took pictures!"

David nodded. "You saw them at the party, and then saw Jill when he had dosed her. At the warehouse, you saw the coyotes bringing her to the room Mark keeps them in until the exchange. She's not dead, Sam. We may still have a chance to help her - but we can't help her without using my plan."

"What do you mean, the room he keeps them in until the exchange? What are you talking about?" Sam was gripping the arms of the chair so tightly her knuckles were white. The IV line taped to the back of her hand looked ready to split her skin stretched tight around it.

"Sam, do you remember ever seeing Tessa? Tall, thin woman, really short haircut?" David motioned with his hands near his temples, then dropped them as Sam nodded. "Tessa works with Mark. She's not a coyote - she's actually an owl, but that's not what's important, at the moment. She has been working with my team to try to take the ring out. Mark is not just dealing with drugs, he's also smuggling bears, which means bears - including werebears - are being killed, supposedly to use the bears' gallbladders and paws medicinally. But on top of the drugs and bears, he's also moving people. I'm not sure where they end up, Tessa's been working that end. She is better equipped to follow those leads than I am."

He had taken a few steps, allowing himself a small space to pace while still trying to minimize the threat Sam felt from him. He glanced at the girls, then shook his head slowly and resumed pacing. "I'm sorry, about the cactus juice he's been slipping you. I honestly thought you were safer with him playing his games with your mind than you would be if he decided he needed you gone - Jill is the first person he's turned over that he actually had a relationship established with. Tessa thinks he's been finding people who have conveniently gotten themselves too wasted to be social because it buys a few days before anyone really starts worrying about them not being around. I don't know, except that he'd been using Jill the same as he has used other girls - as a front to show he's a nice guy - but she was starting to give him trouble. I thought, as Jill's roommate, that the front would extend to you, too. I guess I didn't fully realize how destabilized he's become already."

Kelly, who was sitting next to Sam with one hand on her shoulder, could feel the fine tremors in the taut muscles. She gently squeezed until Sam turned her gaze to her face. "Sam, I know how scary this is. I watched him turn into a beast right in front of me, in the Humanities Building at school. I know that we," Kelly broke off as Sam reached up and grabbed the hand still squeezing her shoulder.

"If Jill is still alive, we have to help her! Oh, God, I thought she was dead!" Tears slipped out of the corners of Sam's eyes and rolled unheeded down her cheeks.

"I would never have left if I thought she needed help." The last words were whispered anguish.

Kelly reached across with her other arm and gathered Sam in a crushing hug. "There was nothing you could do, Sam - not with the drugs he kept giving you. The best thing you could have done for her was to leave - that gave you time for the drugs to leave your system, and it gave David an opening so that, hopefully, he can bring him down before more people get hurt!"

The three of them jumped as the door swung open. Wayne pulled earbuds from his hood and glanced up from his phone as he came through the door, freezing at the sight of Kelly and Sam clutching each other in the chair with David standing in front of them.

"What the?" he trailed off, then turned and lunged for the door.

David grabbed the back of his jacket and pulled him back into the room, slamming the door. He shoved Wayne toward the girls, then backed against the door with his hands raised to hold him off.

Kelly was on her feet. She reached out for Wayne, urging him to listen.

"Wayne! It's okay! We're okay, Wayne," she said, stepping between her brother and David, holding a hand up to each to motion them to stop.

Wayne looked from Kelly's face to David's and back, then to Sam and back at Kelly. Anger and confusion rolled across his face. "What's going on?" He bit out.

Kelly blew out a breath, then put her hands down. "Wayne, this is David. David, Wayne," she motioned between them as she made the introduction. "David is trying to take out Mark's smuggling ring, and we," she motioned to herself and Sam, "are going to help him."

CHAPTER FORTY

Standing to the side of the window in the hardware store two doors from the coffee shop he was supposed to meet her in, Mark watched Kelly walk down the sidewalk toward the crosswalk, a small canvas tote bag loosely hung over one shoulder. She shivered slightly in her jacket and glanced at her watch. She chanced a quick look behind her. Turning back to face the street, she stepped onto the crosswalk and in front of the oncoming car.

The squeal of brakes broke through the cold air. Mark watched Kelly's body roll up on the hood of the car, hit the windshield, and drop off the side of the gray Toyota. The driver of the car, wearing a hoodie sweatshirt and sunglasses, hit the gas and sped away from campus. The driver tapped the brakes as he hung a right on the main road and was soon lost around the next corner.

Mark stayed behind a display of shovels, eyes narrowed as he watched the students getting out of classes in buildings closest to the sidewalk rush toward Kelly's body, crumpled on the sidewalk. He saw that David was among the first to reach her. Within minutes a police cruiser and ambulance were rolling up to the area. Mark watched as David and the other students backed away, waved back by the police officer. Paramedics jumped out of the ambulance and approached the body. One of them knelt on the grass near Kelly's body and reached to touch her neck, then began performing chest compressions while the other man grabbed the police officer to help bring the stretcher over.

David separated himself from the gathered crowd and started toward the coffee shop, a canvas bag in one hand. Walking to the front of the hardware store, Mark opened the door and stepped out as David crossed the street.

"How bad is she hurt?" Mark asked, holding out his hand for the bag.

David grimaced as he passed the bag to Mark and looked at the blood on his hand. Wiping his hand on his jeans, he shook his head. "I don't know, man. There's a lot of blood, and I think her neck might be broken. She's unconscious."

The two turned and watched, unabashed, as the medic performing CPR paused long enough to help work a backboard under the body and move it to the stretcher. The second paramedic and the officer went to either end of the stretcher and lifted, while the first paramedic resumed CPR in an awkward side along position. They moved the stretcher quickly to the back of the ambulance and loaded it into the back, with the first paramedic jumping in and continuing chest compressions. The second medic slammed the doors closed and ran around to the driver's seat. The vehicle rolled into motion a minute later.

Mark glanced down at the bag in his hand. He gingerly shook it open, then reached in with his other hand and withdrew a notebook. Inspecting the bottom corner, which had started to stain with the blood that had soaked through the bag, he dropped the bag to the sidewalk. He inhaled deeply, closing his eyes. He smiled. Opening his eyes, he met David's gaze.

"Well, isn't that tidy. I've got to get back - I've scheduled the shipment for tomorrow night, but there are a few things I need to tie up, first. I'd like it if you could stay here and follow up on this, make sure there are no loose ends. I'll catch up with you for the bus fare," he said.

His gaze traveled the street behind David, watching the ambulance turn the corner, lights flashing, then he glanced back at the crowd. The police officer was talking with a couple of students who were gesturing at the blood on the sidewalk, then pointing the direction the car had driven. Another student was looking around on the ground, and they heard the word, "bag" float across the street. David glanced down as Mark gave a small, shuffling kick and the fabric bag landed under a shrub at the corner of the store.

"Yeah, I can follow up. If she doesn't make it, I may even get back tonight," David said.

Mark nodded. "Yeah, man. If they do manage to revive her, give me a call. Otherwise, I'll see you at the shop. Hey," his split-second pause was barely noticeable. "If you get back tonight, come to the warehouse. There's something I'd like you to see."

David nodded, then turned toward the coffee shop. "I'm going to get a coffee first and warm up. It feels like it's getting ready to rain." He held up his blood-smeared hand. "I want to wash this off, too."

Mark gave a low chuckle. "It's intoxicating! But you go ahead, wash it off. I'm heading out." He lifted a hand in farewell and struck off for the parking lot.

CHAPTER FORTY-ONE

The ambulance took the left turn onto the main street and headed toward town, following the hospital signs. Tyler counted out loud to keep his rhythm for chest compressions, but his hands were no longer centered on Kelly's sternum, but braced on the side of the stretcher, instead. Kelly blew out a loud breath and opened her eyes. "Where are we? Is anyone following us?"

Tyler glanced back out the window. "Nah, nobody following us. Man, that was awesome! John just said to play this like a real fatal, he didn't say the whole freakin' school was going to be there!" He was interrupted by the chime on Kelly's phone. He reached forward to unclick the buckle strapping Kelly to the stretcher so that she could reach her phone and sat back on the bench to give his arms a rest.

Kelly flicked to the message that had come through. "OK, we've got to keep it up for a few more minutes - the guy just left the parking lot. Keep an eye out for a gray car." She set the phone down on her chest and glanced up at Tyler's face. "You weren't kidding when you said the CPR wouldn't feel good!"

"John said it needed to be believable! I was only partially compressing - just enough to make it look real, hopefully not enough to hurt you. You okay?" He reached forward and grabbed her wrist, assessing her pulse as she nodded.

Kelly closed her eyes and prayed their ruse would work. She could feel the blood soaking her t-shirt against her skin and tried not to breathe in the metallic smell. David had been insistent that they had to use real blood in the blood squibs secured under her jacket to make the scene realistic because Mark would be able to smell the difference. He had scoured the area looking for a "vampire bank," but then realized that even if he could locate it, he wouldn't be able to make contact with anyone to be vetted, so wouldn't be able to make the necessary purchase anyway.

"Vampires are not exactly welcome guests, you know? So, they don't usually advertise themselves. If they sold to any Joe who walked off the street, the banks wouldn't be able to maintain cover for long," he had said, before finally settling on a butcher's shop in the North End that sold internal organs. Apparently, meat from the grocery store had already been bled, and the red liquid that seeped out when she cut her steak wasn't really blood, after all, but "cellular fluid," whatever that was. He'd called the shop to see if he could buy blood to make blood pudding. After several redirections, he'd found a store he could get the blood at, but it had taken nearly two hours to make the round trip. The results filled more than enough little baggies with blood to fill the hidden pockets in the jacket Kelly borrowed from the costume closet, designed to allow the squibs to burst with sudden contact and release their contents as though her body had truly broken.

Kelly concentrated on taking shallow breaths through her mouth, trying to calm her gag reflex from reacting to the odor and the thought of being coated in some poor animal's blood.

"Dude, you said a gray car? A gray Honda is coming up behind us," Matt called from the driver's seat.

"OK, guys, just stay on point. Drive right up to the hospital like you're bringing in a real victim," Kelly urged, then fell quiet, feverishly praying for God's protection. She could hear Tyler moving on the bench next to her as he resumed compressions on the edge of the stretcher, and prayed that the ruse would be enough to convince Mark of the reality of her death.

She felt the ambulance slow and round a corner, then pick up speed again.

"If you had a real victim of a car crash you thought was dead, you would do CPR the whole way to the hospital?" Kelly asked.

"The whole way," Tyler said. "Once we start, unless the person starts breathing on their own, we don't stop until a doc tells us to."

He paused and squeezed an airbag near her face, then resumed his position and started compressing the stretcher again. After a minute, he slumped back in his seat. "OK, so the gray car took the left to head toward the highway. I vote we pull in near the ambulance bay, park at the side, and get a coffee. Sound good? Matt?"

"Sounds good! We'll have to be quick, though, I told Jim I thought the training exercise would take less than two hours, and we're over an hour already. We have to have the bus back and ready to roll again."

Kelly's phone pinged again. She unlocked the screen and checked the text.

"Coffee's on me, guys, but I need help with one more thing. I need a picture of me, dead. Where would a body be after the person was declared dead?"

"In the morgue, but I can't see them letting us in there just to take a picture. That definitely tips the wacko scale," Tyler said. He was sitting back on the seat again, looking at Kelly with a quizzical expression. "I thought this was for a movie?"

"Oh, yeah - it's for the movie poster," Kelly improvised. "It doesn't have to be in the morgue, that would be a little creepy, actually. Can we just take it on a stretcher in a quiet hallway, though? I mean, I could wait for one of the film guys to show up, but this is gross." She gestured at her bloody torso. "If I don't have to wait, I can get cleaned up faster."

Tyler smiled at her wrinkled nose. "How'd you manage to get roped into doing one of John's movies, anyway? I thought you were usually putting the costumes on other people?"

Kelly smiled ruefully. "I used to think I wanted to be a stunt actress. I learned how to stage a few stunts, like getting hit by a car. My lucky day, right?"

They pulled in the ambulance entrance to the hospital, drove around the side of the building, and cut the engine. At Kelly's request, Tyler grabbed a backpack that had ridden on the floor between the front seats and handed it to her. She quickly pulled out a mirror and a small kit with sponges and make-up and began dabbing on some gray and pale blues. "It won't be perfect, but if I'm dead I can't have flushed cheeks, right?"

Tyler watched as she transformed herself. "You're good. I would never think of all those colors being used for skin, especially dead skin."

Kelly peered closely in the mirror to ensure all the edges blended well, then sprayed her face with a finishing spray to make sure the colors didn't smudge. She'd left spatters of blood on her face and added a bruise on one temple to increase the plausibility that she would have died from her injuries. She shoved the makeup kit back into the bag and lay back down on the stretcher.

Tyler reached forward and refastened the belts on the stretcher. "Sorry, but I don't want you falling off while we're moving. I'm going to cover you with this blanket, just to get into the building; otherwise, we'll get hit with a ton of questions. John cleared the movie as a training exercise with our Captain, but I doubt he cleared it with the hospital."

Kelly shook her head. "I'm sure you're right. Let's just get the picture taken, and you guys can scoot."

Kelly felt the stretcher bouncing and jostling as they dropped the wheels and rolled it across the parking lot. Matt kept up a steady stream of instructions for Tyler, using his time to give hints on passing the certification Tyler was studying for. Kelly kept her eyes closed. She heard the doors open automatically as they approached, and the bustle of the emergency room beyond. Matt raised his voice in greeting to someone in the room but steered the stretcher down a hallway instead of into the hive of noise. It took a few minutes and a few turns before they stopped.

"This should work," Matt said.

Kelly opened her eyes. They were in a quiet corridor next to a bathroom door. Bulletin boards on the opposite wall held job postings and safety bulletins. The overhead lights cast a dull yellow glow that didn't quite manage to drive the darkness from the corners of the hallway.

"Perfect! Could you guys use my phone, and take a few shots from different angles? That way we have a better chance at getting something they'll be happy with, and I won't have to redo this makeup," she said.

She handed Tyler the phone after unlocking it and closed her eyes. They quickly flew open again as she felt her hair move.

"Sorry," said Matt, pulling the blanket smooth across her collarbone. "I just thought we should try to get it right."

Kelly nodded and closed her eyes again. After a quiet minute that felt like ten, Tyler was handing her her phone. She swiped to see the photos.

"Yes! These should work! Thank you guys, so much - now can you let me out, and I'll change? Let me give you money for coffee." She fumbled at the bag Tyler had tucked at her feet and pulled out some money.

"Nah, we're good," Matt said, grinning. "I just want to see the movie when he finishes it." He piled the sheets and blanket onto the middle of the stretcher and pushed it back into the main hallway, motioning for Tyler to steer it back up the hall.

Kelly ducked into the bathroom with her bag to change out of the bloodied clothes. Washing her hands, she took out her phone and swiped carefully through the photos, zooming in to make sure that what they sent would be believable. She cropped one picture closer to remove Matt's leg and tweaked the warmth on a couple of them to give more credence to the image of a corpse. Finally satisfied, she sent two pictures to David. While she waited for him to get back to her, she cleaned her face with wet paper towels, doing her best to remove the stage makeup and dried blood. She stripped off her clothes and used more wet paper towels to scrub at her skin, trying to erase the feel of the blood they had used before dressing in Wayne's jeans and baggy sweatshirt she pulled from her backpack. Before leaving the bathroom, she used more paper towels to wipe the sink and floor. It wouldn't do to leave traces of blood around, or she'd cause a panic at the hospital when it was discovered.

Her phone pinged. She glanced at the message then grabbed her bag and left the room. She remembered to pull her baseball cap out of the pack and pull it on before the elevator doors slid open. She was alone on the elevator, but she kept the hat on anyway and pulled her backpack over her shoulders. She hunched her shoulders forward and stuck her hands in her front pockets, doing her best to disguise her posture. If anyone did get on the elevator, she couldn't take a chance of being recognized.

CHAPTER FORTY-TWO

"It went okay," she said again. "David is going to send the photos to him in an hour, and then head back to Bridgeville. We just have to stick to the plan until tonight."

Kelly sat across from her mother in Sam's room at the hospital, exhausted. Her father paced the room in front of the bed. The curtains had been pulled across the windows, darkening the room but making sure no one could see in. Her parents had rushed into the hospital shortly after Kelly had reached Sam's room, distraught. They had been met by a nurse in scrubs who walked them into a back hallway, where she had hugged Kelly's mother before showing her one of the less frequented stairways to take to the third floor. While in the stairwell they had put on baggy sweatshirts, clear glasses, and Kelly's mother had clipped on a ponytail hair extension while her dad had pulled on a baseball cap. Her mother still wore the hairpiece, but the rest of the accessories now lay cluttering the table, having served their purpose of disguise to get them into Sam's room, unrecognized by anyone Mark might have lurking to report back to him.

"How are we supposed to know when this is over?" Her father was a tightly wound ball of energy radiating frustration. It had taken a lot of convincing to get him to go along with the ruse. He'd only finally agreed to do so when Sam had gotten hysterical and threatened to leave the hospital and go back to Bridgeville to find Jill herself.

"I'm not sure, exactly. David said that one of his teammates would be here by supper time," Kelly said. "She's going to move us to the safe spot."

"Dad, come sit down," Sam urged, patting the bed next to her.

He crossed the room and sat, putting his arm around her too-thin shoulders and pulling her close for a hug. Sam was dressed in jeans and a faded blue sweatshirt, her hair combed to the wrong side. She wore foundation makeup with no blush or mascara, giving her a plain, unflattering appearance. None of them had argued with Kelly when she instructed them on their simple disguises. "The easiest way to disappear is just to blend in," she had told them. "We wear plain, average clothes; nothing to draw attention because it's too nice, or too blah," she'd explained. "We change the details in subtle ways: hair, glasses, style. We don't make eye contact if we can manage it. We just try to move under the radar."

They had copied the notebook pages with an app on Kelly's cell phone, which allowed them to take images of the book exactly as it was, including any folded pages or inserted bookmarks, just in case they proved to be important in deciphering the code Mark had used. David had used Kelly's cell phone to send the pages to Amy, one of the agents on his team.

"I can't risk it being on my phone, but I need the other agents to have the information as soon as possible so they can start working on this right away," he had explained. "Plus, this gives you another contact to the team, in case it proves necessary."

The plans had taken a while to hash out last night, even after they had finally convinced Kelly's parents. David had given the agent a pass-phrase to use when she came to pick them up as an added layer of protection. He was capable and competent, and his efficient manner helped to sway Kelly's parents, but Kelly caught his eye and held it. She had seen Mark shift in minutes, had seen the cruel gleam in his eye when he knew he had terrified her. She was sure that David was in far more danger than he was letting them understand. She dropped her gaze. She agreed with his decision to keep some of the details from them - her parents wouldn't knowingly consent to someone else being put in danger for them, even if it was a trained agent.

Now, her mind wandered back to that thought. How much training had David had? What sort of training? How, exactly, would they train agents for work against were-creatures? Who would first have approached him with that suggestion, and how would they have put it? "Hey, don't think I'm insane, but those stories about were-wolves and vampires and all - they aren't just stories. They are real, and we need help controlling them without freaking out the rest of the world. You in?"

Kelly wondered how Wayne was faring, sitting in a class at school knowing that all of this was going on. He hadn't wanted to go to school. David had insisted that it would be less suspicious, especially if Mark had someone else watching the family. As close as David was to the mainstream of Mark's organization, even he didn't know everyone that Mark had working for him. The plan was for Wayne to drive their mother's car to the library after school and wait there until he was picked up.

"I don't want him alone! He could take the bus here," Kelly's mother had suggested, but David had vetoed the idea quickly.

"It's too easy to pick someone up from the bus - if he is being watched and Mark suspects anything, they'll get him before anyone even thinks to call and check in with him," he had said. "If he goes to school and leaves with the rest of the students, he should be safe getting into the car. The library is still in the center of town so they wouldn't have a chance to force him off the road between there and the school, and they won't get suspicious - he's a student, it's the library. They'll likely sit on the car and won't realize he's safe until the library closes."

Kelly knew that Wayne wasn't happy about being kept out of the way, but her parents had been adamant. She and Sam were both legally adults, but Wayne was still in high school, as they had stressed at least three times during the conversation with him the night before.

They all jumped at the sound of a knock just before the door opened. A wiry, middle-aged woman stepped into the room. Her glance swept the room before she spoke into the silence. "David said to say, 'Proverbs 27:12, the prudent see danger and take refuge, but the simple keep going and pay the penalty,'" she said, and held out a leather wallet opened to reveal a badge and ID. "I'm Amy. I've come to take you to the safe house."

Kelly's father strode to the woman, peering at the ID. He looked into her face, comparing it to the image on the ID, then reached to shake her hand. "Can you tell us what's going on? Have you heard from David?"

Amy nodded but gestured instead of answering his questions. "I can fill you in on the way, but it's best if we move quickly. Do you have everything ready to go?"

Kelly grabbed her backpack and helped Sam gather the bags she had packed with her clothes and cards while their father explained about Wayne. Amy nodded. "Yes, David explained," she said. "It was a good decision. We will swing by the library to pick him up before we head out of town."

They moved into the hall and walked to the elevator. Kelly kept her eyes down, and her shoulders rounded. Sam walked between their parents, her father's arm around her shoulders. Amy stepped next to Kelly. She carried one of Sam's bags loosely in her arm. Glancing at her face, Kelly noticed that her eyes moved around the corridor, darting quick peeks past each open door they passed. Though her body language belied it to a casual observer, her sharp eyes demonstrated her heightened vigilance.

"Wait," Amy glanced around as she breathed out the quiet word. She pushed the button for the elevator when she saw a nurse's aide turn the corner. As the aide pushed a door open and left the hall, Amy turned to face them. "You three," she indicated Sam and their parents, "take the elevator downstairs. Kelly and I will take the stairs down. There is a shuttle van outside - don't get in until you see me. We'll reach it at the same time, but it will look accidental to anyone else."

The elevator door slid open. The cab was empty. Nodding quickly to Sam and her parents, Amy pushed the door to the stairwell open and urged Kelly through before following her. The door swung shut behind them as they descended the stairs. "Five people is too many to hide easily," Amy explained, cocking her head to listen and peering up the staircase at the same time. "An overabundance of caution is better than not."

They reached the lobby with no issues. Kelly saw a few people standing in line for the coffee shop, but the large crowd they had encountered on their first foray from Sam's room was nowhere to be found. She glanced at the clock on the wall - it was nearly six. Getting late for casual visitors, she guessed. She followed Amy out the door, keeping her eyes trained on the floor, and almost bumped into her when she stopped. Looking up quickly, Kelly saw that they had reached the shuttle van. Amy indicated to stow the bags in the back of the vehicle, then crossed behind and opened the rear drivers' side door. Kelly climbed in and moved to the rear as her parents and Sam reached the side closest to the building. They jumped in as Amy spoke with the driver, then climbed in through the door behind his seat. Kelly wasn't sure anyone paying attention would have been fooled, but she didn't see anyone paying attention, either.

The ride to the library was uneventful. Kelly texted Wayne when they pulled up to the side staircase. Wayne had parked the car in the main parking lot across the street from the front entrance, so it was unlikely that anyone would be staking out the side doors. He jogged down the stairs and hurried to the van, sliding into the seat as his father opened the door from the inside.

"What happened? Did it work?" The questions tumbled out of him even as he reached for the door and slid it shut. "I was going crazy in there - you could have texted me!" He twisted in his seat to look at Kelly searchingly. "You okay?"

Kelly nodded. "It went okay. He left and told David to make sure I'm dead." Kelly paused, her mouth pulling into a curious frown as she realized how that sounded. Her eyes flicked to her mother, sitting next to Sam, and she quickly went on, "so we took a couple of pictures for proof, and now David is going back, too." She met Wayne's eyes. "I'm sorry, but I didn't dare text you. Just in case."

Wayne grimaced but nodded his understanding.

Amy cleared her throat. "Okay, here's what I can fill you in on. We were able to figure out at least some of the code Mark has been using - enough to know his delivery schedule for the next couple of shipments." She looked at Kelly. "That was good thinking, to shoot pictures of all the bookmarks, too. Some of those figured into his cipher."

When she did not immediately speak again, Dad broke the silence. "And? What does all of this mean for us? When can we go back home?" His mouth opened for another question but Sam put her hand on his arm and leaned forward, interrupting his flow.

"Does it say what happened to Jill?"

Amy eyes slanted toward Sam's face and away. "We haven't been able to translate the whole thing, yet. We aren't sure what that says about Jill. What this does mean for your family is that you aren't safe until Mark is stopped. We'll be better able to give you a timetable after tonight." She looked back and forth between Mom and Dad. "David said you had family in another state? It might mean going for a visit. It might mean more than that - we really don't know, yet. We should be at the safe house in about an hour."

She moved to sit in the front passenger seat, leaving the family to sit in stunned silence.

CHAPTER FORTY-THREE

I t had been two days since the scene of the accident, two days since they had had any contact with "the real world," as Wayne had started to call the rest of their lives. Mom and Dad had both called into work and taken leave for a family emergency, saying they were not sure how long it would take. Mom had called in to excuse Wayne from classes, too. Mom had tried to get him to agree to work on his assignments since he had his books with him, but Wayne had rolled his eyes.

The safe house turned out to be a condo in a large 55 and older mobile home park. Amy had turned them over to Gladys and Richard, the older couple who rented the home.

"Remember, appearances can be deceiving," she said before they got out of the van.

Gladys was just over five feet tall, with plump features and a warm smile. She had made them all turn over their cell phones before walking through the door.

"You cannot be serious!" Dad had argued, but she smiled sweetly, hand outstretched and toes tapping as she blocked his entrance. His frown deepened the lines on his forehead as he finally handed his over.

"This wouldn't be a safe house if we allowed unskilled access to the web," she said, still smiling.

It turned out that her smile hid a backbone of steel. Even Richard, who towered over her at almost six feet, rolled his eyes on occasion but meekly did as she directed.

"Doesn't do any good to argue," he said. "I've been on the receiving end of her quills once, and I never want to be again. Best to just do as she says."

"What do you mean, quills?" Kelly has asked. "As in, porcupine?"

Richard just lifted one corner of his mouth. Kelly wasn't sure if that was agreement, or laughing at her. They didn't give much away.

Because they weren't allowed to use their phones, and there wasn't a computer available to use, they spent hours in front of the television. Kelly quickly tired of the courtroom drama that Gladys favored, and the second television in the guest bedroom was not connected to cable. She found herself perusing the couple's bookshelves for a diversion. She ran a finger along the spines of a row of romances, finally pulling out a book with a female pirate on the cover.

"Richard thinks he can learn about the female mind by reading those," Gladys said, coming up to stand beside Kelly. "I've tried explaining that they set unreal expectations for women, but he thinks that if it's in writing, it must be real."

Kelly smiled, sliding the pirate book back into its space on the shelf. "What do you like to read?" She asked.

Gladys reached up to the top shelf, where Kelly hadn't even looked yet, and pulled down a book of fairy tales. "This isn't your Grimm Brothers' book," she said. She sized Kelly up. "I'd say start with this one, and if you're still interested, I've got one on therianthropes. I have a feeling you might need it."

Kelly took the offered book and made her way to the couch with mixed emotions. She was part way through the first story - a version of Sleeping Beauty where a king assaulted the sleeping woman and impregnated her - when the front door opened.

• • • •

"JILLY!"

Sam bounded from the chair she had been curled up watching Judge Judy in and wrapped her arms around the slender girl who had followed the agents into the house. Jill returned the hug, tears streaming their way down her face. Her wrists, exposed beyond the sleeves of her coat, bore dark bruises. Her hair was stringy and hung limply around her face.

"Oh, honey," Mom cried, and gathered them both in her arms.

David walked over to Kelly, avoiding the knot of weeping women in the center of the room, and sat in the seat her mother had just vacated. His smile was tired.

"We got him," he said. "We didn't get as far up the chain as we hoped, but we got Mark, his crew, and the guy he was making his delivery to."

"But, I thought it was about catching the bigger fish," Kelly said. "What changed?"

David gazed at the women in the center of the room. His forearms were resting on his knees, his hands clasping and unclasping.

"The ledger you gave us. We were able to decipher it. It turns out that the drugs - the cactus juice, the peyote, even the bear parts - those were actually the low hanging fruit. Mark's big payout was actually from trafficking people," he said. He stared down at his hands.

Kelly stared at Jill, Sam, and her mom for a long minute. She turned to search David's face. "Trafficked for what?" She asked quietly. She had more questions, a lot more, but she stopped herself.

David shook his head, indicating the women with a quick nod of his head. They were separating and looking around for seats. Sam dragged a straight chair over to the side of the armchair she had been sitting in, then drew Jill over to the armchair. Sam perched on the straight chair, holding Jill's hand with both of her own.

"I am so, so sorry," Sam said, emotion making her voice raw.

Jill shook her head vehemently, tears continuing their silent streams over her cheeks. She pulled Sam's hand up to her face and leaned against it, eyes closing.

Sam looked at David and the other agent. Her eyes asked the question she didn't voice.

David cleared his throat, but the other agent stepped forward and spoke first.

"I'm Agent Moore. I work with Agents Bryant and Bupo. We were able to use the information gathered from the ledger you had appropriated to intercept a vehicle heading to the delivery point. The vehicle held 17 people who had been held captive for various lengths of time," he said, keeping his eyes averted from Jill's tear-stained face as he delivered his summary. "The vehicle waiting at the rendezvous spot had been modified to add separate compartments for each of the victims. It quickly became apparent that this was not the first such transaction these operatives had been engaged in. Your intervention was timely, and of great importance." He nodded at Sam and Kelly, as though bestowing honor on each of them. He turned toward Dad, who had moved to sit on the arm of the chair so that Mom could have the seat. "We have processed the ledger and the warehouse, and believe that all the ends of this side of the chain have been accounted for. It should be safe for you to return to your home and your lives now."

Dad turned his face toward the ceiling, eyes closed, and squeezed Mom's hand. "What about this Mark, the one who threatened our family - what's going to happen to him?"

Agent Moore cleared his throat. "Mr. Jacobs attempted to escape the area and fought against our agents with an armed show of force, which ultimately resulted in Mr. Jacobs sustaining life-threatening injuries that he has succumbed to. Your family is safe."

"Praise God!" Dad whispered, shaking his head and exhaling slowly. He stood and grasped Agent Moore's hand, pumping it with relief. Turning to the driveway, he swiveled around to look at Agent Moore again. "We don't have a car. We came in the van - how will we get home?"

Agent Moore was nodding. "Yes, sir, we are aware that you were transported to this spot and are prepared to bring you back to your vehicles. We have called for a shuttle van to pick you up."

Richard stepped into the living room from outdoors. Kelly hadn't realized he had been outside but now saw him tucking away a cell phone. He caught her looking at his pocket and gave his little half-smile, adding a wink so quick she wasn't sure she'd actually seen it.

"Jill? If you're ready, I'll take you now," he said, his voice gentle.

"What do you mean, you'll take her? Where is she going?" Sam demanded, gripping her friend's hand more tightly. "Can't she come with us?"

Richard smiled at Sam sadly. "Jill needs a little more help right now than you can give her," he said. "And her parents have been notified that she's been found. They'll be meeting us at the hospital."

Sam's face fell. She leaned in close to Jill. "I'm going to come visit, Jilly. And we're going to be okay. Okay?"

Jill gave her a weak smile. The tears had slowed considerably, though an occasional drop did roll down her cheek. She nodded and accepted Richard's hand to stand up. Kelly thought she looked frail. After watching Richard help her out the door and down the front steps, Kelly turned and caught David watching her.

"Agent Bryant?" Agent Moore stood waiting.

David jumped, clearly caught at not paying attention. "Right, sorry," he said, grinning slightly at Kelly as he flushed. "It's been a long couple of days." He stood, reaching into his back pocket for his wallet. He pulled out a business card. He passed it to Kelly, who was still seated. "There will be more questions. We'll be in touch, but in the meantime, don't hesitate to call if you need to."

Kelly took the card reflexively. She stood as he walked away, as did the rest of the family. David shook hands with everyone on his way out the door, thanking each for their patience and participation in the ruse that helped them fool Mark. Kelly glanced down at the card but put it in her pocket without reading it.

The next 20 minutes were a whirlwind of gathering belongings - including their cell phones, which Gladys made them promise to wait to power up until they were out of the community. She saw Kelly stretch to put the book she had borrowed back on the bookshelf and stopped her. "I've got two more copies of that book somewhere here," she said. "Take that one and read it through. If you ever get tired of it, you can get it back to David, and he'll see that I get it back."

Kelly thanked her and tucked the book into her backpack. She wondered at Gladys' odd manner of speaking but put it down to being from a different generation.

Kelly chose the middle row of seats in the van, letting her parents and Sam sit together in the front row. Wayne grabbed the last row, turning sideward to lean against the window and stretching his legs out on the seat. He held his cell phone in his hand, but, true to his word, didn't turn it on until they cleared the gate to the community. Kelly turned hers on, too. She was curious to see what she had missed. While she waited for it to go through its startup cycle, she remembered the card in her pocket and pulled it out.

It was a business card from a car rental agency. Kelly frowned. It would have been odd to have business cards when he couldn't carry a badge in case he was suspected, but to give her a card from someone else? She flipped it over. There, in pencil, in impossibly neat writing, David had written his name and cell phone number, followed by four words: Think about joining us.

Kelly stared at the card. Her phone vibrated in her hand, then again, and again. She glanced again at the card, then tucked it back into her pocket. Maybe she would, she thought, as she swiped at the phone to see her notifications. Maybe she would.

From the author:

I hope you have enjoyed the first of the Fighting in Shadows series. For a free companion short story giving a glimpse of the background of one of our main characters, sign up for my newsletter at https://mailchi.mp/e8f9334f8c35/fightinginshadows. You can also visit my Facebook page at www.facebook.com/fightinginshadows[1]. Hope to see you there!

---

1.   http://www.facebook.com/fightinginshadows

About the Author

Piper Dow writes contemporary fantasy, paranormal, new adult fiction. She enjoys all things that instill a sense of wonder into the everyday.

Made in the USA
Middletown, DE
14 July 2019